HUNTER

The Arcane Rebellion Book Two

Written by Denis James

Legal Stuff

Dedications & Acknowledgements

Within life, you cross paths with many different people. Each person you cross paths with is meant to shape you, to grow you, and to develop you into the person you are today.

This book is dedicated to every single person I have crossed paths with. If we've met, even briefly, I thank you for helping shape me into the man I've become. This wouldn't be possible without you.

Notably, this includes the people who have done right by me. The people who have done wrong. The people who have moved on. And the people who are keeping me strong.

Thank you all.

Much love,

Denis James

Table of Contents

Chapter One: Hunter's Painful Choice

Snow was falling slowly this early December morning. Winter was fast approaching as usual in the town of Jefferson. A petite town that was close enough to the big city to get there for a day trip, but not close enough to be disturbed by the day-to-day hustle and bustle of the crowds. It had truly been a marvelous place to live until the catastrophe that had plagued the town a few months back: a fire that had started in the local high school, and spread to other parts of the community before it had gone out of its own volition.

Firefighters and arson investigators were unable to explain the cause of the fire, or its abrupt end. The water, extinguishers, and other tools that first responders had used against the fire had done nothing to put an end to it. It had destroyed the school, had decimated several nearby houses and neighborhoods, and had wreaked havoc on the local wildlife population. By the time the fire had finally been extinguished, it was too late. No less than two hundred lives had been lost—students and staff at the school, parents who had rushed in to try to save their children, and neighbors who lived near the school had already perished a horrible death.

Several people had moved away from Jefferson at this point. For one, it was too painful for them to continue living so close to where they had lost loved ones. For two, the town was falling on tough economic times; many of the shopkeepers had closed their doors and moved closer to the city. A small group of people continued to live in the town though, and an effort to rebuild the school had begun. Progress was slow; the state was reluctant to provide taxpayer funding for a school that would, at this point, only benefit a few dozen families. The group continued their battle for the school, but with more people leaving the town every week, things looked bleak for the group.

However, there was talk about a new resident of Jefferson. A strong, young man of Mexican descent, medium build, with short dark hair and piercing black eyes had moved into one of the abandoned houses only weeks prior. It was quite unusual for the town of Jefferson to have a new resident, particularly in these trying times. Ordinarily, it would be huge news to have a new neighbor, particularly a non-white person, though now it seemed there were much more pressing matters at hand for the residents of the town. Most of the residents hadn't really spoken to the man much, though a few of them had seen him out and about on his property. A small house that had belonged to two of the local town's teachers, the couple had apparently left him their home. There was speculation about the relationship this man had with the teachers, though nothing was confirmed, and no one in the town cared enough about the new resident to question him.

Therefore, when the man exited the house that morning, he was unsurprised to find no one around. His new home was surrounded by trees, cut off from the road and other properties. There was a long driveway extending out to the road, which would take several minutes to walk to. The property was vast and well cared for. The man looked up at the snow falling as he exited the house, smiling. He loved the snow, and the cold; Christmas was truly his favorite time of year.

The man stood in silence for a few minutes, watching the snow fall around him. When a voice shouted from inside the house, a hoarse voice that sounded like it came from someone who hadn't spoken in several months' time:

"HUNTER!'"

Hunter Diaz sighed; Tobias Thornfield was calling for him again. He and Tobias had been best friends for years when Hunter decided he wanted to be more than friends. Tobias, however, didn't seem to be interested. This broke Hunter's heart, and resulted in Hunter leaving him for a year, leaving Tobias and the Bellwater Mages behind. He had been taken in by the Arcane Rebellion, founded by Sabrina Braithwraite and Lucien Rodson. Those two were the leaders of the Rebellion, and they also happened to be leading the Bellwater Mages now.

"What is it, Toby?"

"I told you not to call me that! And get in here! I'm not done talking to you!"

Hunter turned around and walked back into the house, his eyebrows raised.

"What?"

"You...you...I can't believe you are doing this! You attacked me, attacked the school I was working in. Then you attacked Bellwater. What's gotten into you?!"

"I opened my eyes, Toby," Hunter explained carefully, with the air of someone explaining something simple to a small child. "I opened them wide, and I saw the Bellwater Mages for what they were: weak, disorganized, and being owned by Aurora Wildwood. And you've been here for about a month."

Aurora Wildwood was the former leader of the Bellwater Mages, and Hunter's reason for leaving the group. She was–there was no other word for it–*bossy* and had taken it upon herself to micromanage every move made by the other mages of Bellwater. All of them–Toby, Agatha O'Connor, Matilda Carrington–stood by and allowed it to happen. But not him. And not Sabrina or Lucien. They made their own futures, their own destinies, and Aurora Wildwood wasn't going to tell them what they could or couldn't do.

"Aurora wasn't trying to micromanage us," Tobias replied firmly. "She was just looking out for our best interests."

"Oh, is she now?" asked Hunter. "And how is that working out for you?"

Tobias didn't answer, he was too busy glaring at Hunter.

"I beat you," Hunter said quietly. "I beat you in a duel, and now you're my prisoner. You're at my mercy, Tobias."

"What are you going to do with me?" asked Tobias, even more quietly.

The two men stared at each other, as though sizing each other up. Then Hunter whispered back, "I still haven't decided."

"You need to make your decision quickly," Tobias replied, at a much more natural volume. Hunter was a little taken aback. "I know the Rebellion has ordered my death. Are you going to do it? Are you going to kill me, Hunter? Or are you going to betray them?"

4

"Be quiet, Tobias!" Hunter snapped. "I'll...I'll think of something."

"Perhaps," Tobias retorted, looking skeptically at Hunter. "Hopefully by then it's not too late for you to save yourself."

"And what do you mean by that?"

"You're kind of between a rock and a hard place here, Hunter. You either kill me—which would, I don't need to tell you, not make anyone at Bellwater happy. Or you let me live—which would anger everyone with the Rebellion. The time has come for you to decide. Where do your loyalties lie? With me? Or with them?"

"I am late to a meeting," Hunter replied shortly. "I need to leave you now." He verified that Tobias was still chained to the wall; he was. The chains would prevent Tobias from using magic, blocking off his powers. "You stay here. I'll be back soon."

Tobias glared at him as he left the house, closing the door on the way out. Hunter began the long walk up the driveway, where he would teleport to the Rebellion's headquarters found on the coast. He had prevented the use of teleportation anywhere on his property, which meant he had to walk up the driveway to the road in order to leave.

As Hunter walked, he thought long and hard about what Tobias had said. "Where do your loyalties lie? With me? Or with them?" How could he possibly choose? On the one hand, Tobias had been his best friend–very nearly his lover. On the other hand, the Rebellion had taken him in at his lowest point, after being turned down by Tobias. Hunter's internal struggle continued as he walked, until he finally reached the road and was able to teleport.

Hunter teleported directly into a dimly lit room with no windows or doors. The room housed a round table with eight chairs, all but one of which were occupied. In the middle of the table was a basin filled with water; this was used for scrying or looking at another person or location from a distance. This room, Hunter knew, was the meeting room for the Arcane Rebellion.

"Good evening, Hunter."

A tall, blonde woman with dark red lipstick and her hair up in a ponytail had spoken. This was Sabrina Braithwaite, the leader of the Arcane Rebellion. She was seated directly across from where Hunter had appeared. To her right sat her boyfriend, Lucien Rodson, who was middle-aged and chubby. Lucien was looking at Sabrina with so much love and affection it physically pained Hunter.

To Lucien's right was another slightly overweight man in his mid-late forties: Ted. Hunter didn't know his last name; last names were somewhat insignificant to the Arcane Rebellion. Only Sabrina and Lucien knew everyone's last names; indeed, they knew everything there was to know about each of their members. Hunter had been on missions with Ted in the past, and he knew that Ted specialized in fire magic. He also knew that Ted had experience in legal affairs, having worked as an attorney in the past.

To Ted's right was a brown-haired girl named Elena, and to her right was her twin sister Lyra. Hunter didn't know much about them other than he had burned down their school. He was rather shocked to see that Sabrina had permitted them into this meeting; he was under the impression they were undergoing intense therapy and a strict training regimen. To their right was the boy Darian, whom Tobias had resurrected several weeks ago. That was a topic that they had not properly addressed, thought Hunter. He would have to make sure to ask Tobias about that when he returned to him. Then he remembered that Tobias was angry with him.

To the right of Darian sat a girl named Marina, a young woman in her early twenties with long, vivid blue hair. Hunter had never really collaborated with her, though he knew Ted disliked her. Now that he came to think of it, he wasn't sure Ted really liked anyone. Marina specialized in water magic, which was rather uncommon for the Arcane Rebellion. Most of the members specialized in fire, though it was handy to have some variety in their ranks.

Hunter took his seat—to the left of Sabrina—and everyone turned to face him. The teenagers, he noticed, were glaring at him similar to how Tobias had done. He turned away from them and faced Sabrina.

"Now, Hunter. At our last meeting, you informed us that Tobias Thornfield had been killed, and his body had been disposed of."

"That is correct," Hunter replied, politely.

"Where is the body?"

"Gone."

"Gone where, exactly?"

Hunter hesitated; he had expected this to come up, but still didn't want to answer the question. "I buried it," he replied after a few seconds.

"Where?"

"In that clearing by Bellwater Academy. The last place those fools will ever think to look."

Sabrina stared at him. He thought for a moment that she would yell at him. But then she threw her head back and laughed.

"That is…almost too perfect, Hunter! Of course, you're correct; they would never think to look in the most obvious place. Especially as you buried him!"

Lucien, Marina, and Ted joined in Sabrina's laughter. Ted elbowed Elena in the chest, and she gasped, then started chuckling as well. Her sister and Darian joined in, though with reluctance.

The laughter died away after a few minutes. Sabrina looked significantly cheerier than she had prior to the start of the meeting.

"Well, Hunter has done his part of the mission. Taking out Tobias was an integral part of our plan…but certainly not the only one. Lucien and I have done our parts." She nodded to Lucien, who stood up.

"We are delighted to announce that Sabrina has been named leader of the Bellwater Mages!"

Marina and Ted gasped at this news; they clearly felt it was incredible that the Rebellion had managed to carry out such a task. Hunter didn't say anything but smiled at Sabrina and Lucien. The children, Hunter noticed, sat in silence, not making eye contact with anyone in the room. He wondered what was going on in their minds, what they were thinking. Were they happy with the Rebellion's success? Aurora Wildwood had previously attacked one of them with a flower and nearly strangled her to death with its vine-like stem. Or perhaps they were reluctant to work with the Rebellion, which was understandable given Hunter's own role in burning their school and community to the ground. He supposed he would need to do a little bit of digging into their minds at some point. For now, he turned his attention back to Sabrina.

"So, what's our next step?" asked the girl named Marina excitedly, her blue hair sparkling in the firelight.

"Well, we cannot simply command the Bellwater fools to yield to us," said Sabrina simply. "That would be too easy, I'm afraid. No, we will have to dispose of them. And I think it would be best to dispose of them one at a time, in secret."

She turned to Lucien. "Dear," she said sweetly, with a note of honey in her words, "have you figured out a plan?"

"We have two options, my love," he said, smiling at her like a child at Christmas. "We can either take a stealthy approach and attack the mages one at a time, or we can lead a full-on assault on the academy."

Marina frowned at this. "But I thought we wanted to have them join us? If we kill them, how can they do so? Are we going to resurrect them all?"

"No," said Sabrina sweetly. "No, my dear, we won't need

to. We won't need to kill all of them; only the most…troublesome. The ones who will never join us no matter what we do, say, or ask. Starting with Aurora."

She turned to the twins and Darian. "And I think," she said slowly, "that Elena should be the one to do it. Revenge is a dish best served cold, don't you think?"

Elena looked at her, startled.

"But, Ms. Braithwaite, I don't–"

"No, my dear. Call me Sabrina. No need for such formalities here."

"Er–Sabrina. I don't think I can. I don't know any magic, I just–"

"There's no reason to worry!" exclaimed Sabrina, smiling widely. "Hunter is going to teach you magic!"

Hunter, who had been daydreaming silently and only half listening to this conversation, was shaken out of his stupor at these words.

"I'm doing what now?" asked Hunter sharply.

"You want *him* to teach me?" asked Elena angrily; it was clear that she had been expecting someone else to teach her.

"Yes, my dear. What element would you like to learn first?"

"Fire," said Elena quickly. "I can burn down every damn flower I see." She shuddered at the thought of the sunflower wrapped around her neck.

"And I want lightning," Lyra interjected quickly. Sabrina looked surprised at this.

"You—er—don't want the same as your sister?"

"No. I want to learn about lightning magic. Just because we're twins doesn't mean we're the same person, you know."

"Well, none of us specialize in that element here, though I suppose Lucien could join forces with you a little bit."

Lucien smiled at Lyra. "It'll be my pleasure to teach you."

"And how about you, my brave boy?" Sabrina asked Darian sweetly. Darian looked startled.

"Well...I was thinking of Earth magic, actually."

Elena and Lyra stared at him.

"Why?" they asked in unison, suspiciously.

"If I specialize in Earth magic, and the two of you specialize in fire and lightning magic," Darian explained, "None of the Bellwater Mages can use their magic against us again. Remember, we're immune to our own form of magic."

There was a look of realization on the girls' faces upon this statement, and Hunter thought he knew what they were thinking. If one of them specialized in fire, one in storms (water, wind, and lightning all had some overlap into storm magic), and one in Earth magic, they would hypothetically be nearly unstoppable by any magical force. Fire mages couldn't be burned by fire, and storm mages couldn't be hurt by the elements. Therefore, it stood to reason that having all three branches of magic would make one master of the arcane arts. Of course, this wasn't fool proof. It took an exceptional level of skill and experience in the said branch of magic to build up true resistance to it. Many mages never quite reached that level, even after years of practice. Hunter rather doubted they knew that, of course. But he was still reluctantly impressed with the foresight they seemed to display.

"Hmmm," pondered Sabrina. "Well, I suppose I could teach you a thing or two about Earth magic, though I'm not an expert. Hunter, you're with Elena. Lucien, you're with Lyra. And Darian, you're with me." She smiled sweetly at him. He gave a weak smile back.

"Now, please listen closely because I don't want to repeat myself here. No one. I repeat, no one. Is to attack the Bellwater Mages or the Academy. Lucien and I will manage things there. You are all excused. Children, I expect you to begin your studies first thing in the morning."

The mages all got up. Elena walked up to Hunter at the end of the meeting.

"Well, I guess you're my teacher." She was glaring at him.

Hunter sighed. He supposed he should have expected this, though it would be troublesome he feared.

"If you have something you'd like to say to me, now's the time–"

"Fuck you. That's what I have to say."

12

Elena stormed away, returning to her sister and Darian. Hunter scoffed.

"Be ready tomorrow morning, Elena. We start training first thing in the morning! Cruise ship warehouse!" He called after her. Then he turned around and teleported back out of the room.

Hunter arrived back at his house in Jefferson and began the short walk up to his house. He was thinking about everything that had happened at the meeting; how he had lied to the Rebellion to save Tobias. It seemed he had made his choice: he was choosing Tobias over them.

He walked into the house to see Tobias lying in the middle of the living room floor. He wasn't sleeping; he looked up as Hunter entered the room.

"You're back."

Tobias did not sound happy to see Hunter. The man sighed.

"Yes, I'm back."

"So, you must have told them I'm dead."

Hunter turned away from Tobias.

"Ha! So, you did!"

"I did."

"What are you going to do? Hide me here until the end of

time?"

"I don't know!" Hunter snapped, turning back to face Tobias. "I don't know what I'm going to do, Toby! This never would've happened if you had just–"

He stopped and turned away from Tobias again.

"You're in a load of trouble here potentially, Hunter," Tobias explained gently. "You can still let me go. It's not too late. We'll figure something out, we always do."

"I'm afraid it's not that simple."

"Why not?"

"Because..." Hunter froze and turned back around again. "Because I can't protect you."

"I don't need your protection, Hunter."

"Oh, yes you do."

"You don't think I can handle myself? Unchain me, and let's have a fair fight. No innocent people around for you to use this time."

The tension between the two men at this was palpable; Hunter could feel it. He hesitated, not wanting to upset his best friend. But it appeared they were long past that. Tobias turned away from him.

"What would you have had me do, Hunter?"

"What?"

"I stopped you before you could finish. You had said, this never would have happened if I had just. Done what, exactly?"

Hunter snarled at him. "You never should've trusted Aurora."

Tobias sighed. "Not this again. How many times do we need to talk about this? She helped us, Hunter. She helped us out of a tight spot on more than one occasion."

"And what has she done since, Tobias? Strangled a student? Demolished a town? Killed an entire police force?"

"She wouldn't have had to if you hadn't forced her hand."

"What do you mean?"

"You attacked me, Hunter. You and your…strange fixation over me. What is that, by the way? Why are you so obsessed with me?"

"I'm not obsessed!" Hunter's squawk of indignation was as good as a confession. Tobias raised his eyebrows at him. Hunter sighed in defeat. "I just…I never really got over you."

Tobias sighed again. "You need to."

"You think I don't know that?"

"No, I think you do. It's easier said than done though, I suppose." Tobias paused for a moment, then said quietly, "Not sure what exactly there is of me to love though."

"What's not to love, Toby?"

For the first time, Tobias turned a slight shade of pink at these words. Hunter smirked.

"You're blushing."

"Yeah. Anyway, moving past that. What are we going to do?"

"Nothing. We're going to lay low for a while."

"You realize people will be looking for me, right?"

Hunter snorted. "You mean the Bellwater Mages? They won't find you."

Tobias blanched, then turned away from Hunter. Hunter noticed, however. Despite everything he had done, Tobias's well-being was still at the front of his mind.

"That's not a bad thing, Toby. It means you and I can be together!"

"Yeah…that's great, Hunter."

Chapter Two: Someday When I Stop Loving You

Hunter woke up early the next morning. He and Tobias had returned to the cottage's small bedroom. He turned over and stared at the man sleeping by his side. Tobias had freshly showered, and was wearing a clean t-shirt (one of Hunter's favorites) and a pair of sweatpants Hunter used for jogging. At least in theory; the sweatpants were actually brand new, since Hunter never did get around to taking up jogging. Tobias was snoozing; Hunter didn't want to move too much in case it woke him up. Tobias seemed to awaken very easily these days. Hunter supposed that when you're being held captive, it is hard to stay asleep and to feel safe.

While Hunter felt he was doing the right thing–getting Tobias away from the Bellwater Mages, and especially away from Aurora–he couldn't help but feel a pang of regret and sorrow at his actions.

Is it possible I'm going about this all wrong? He kept asking himself. But he shook his head at the thought of that; it was far too late to go back on his actions. Less than a month had passed since he had captured Tobias at Bellwater Clearing. He recalled how easy it was to do so. Tobias's greatest weakness was always his uncanny need to protect those he cared for. By attacking while that Fox kid was in the area, Tobias had had his guard down. From there, it was easy for Hunter to swoop in and capture Tobias.

However, his job was far from done. Hunter's new task

required him to keep Tobias out of sight, out of mind. He needed to make sure Sabrina, Lucien, and the other members of the Arcane Rebellion didn't catch on to what he was doing. This was going to be a problem. Having to train Elena Wilkins in fire magic wasn't his idea of a good time even on a good day but having to do so while trying to keep the fact he was holding Tobias prisoner a secret would be damn near impossible.

Hunter continued to stare lovingly at Tobias. He had never really gotten over him. Tobias had turned him down flat on more than one occasion, claiming that they were "just friends" and that he had no feelings beyond friendship. But Hunter had more than that. He couldn't help it; Tobias was so *needy,* and Hunter was someone who could give Tobias everything he wanted and more. Hunter knew Tobias struggled with clinical depression. He knew Tobias' triggers, his symptoms, and what helped him the most throughout his battle with his mental health issues. At the time, Hunter had done what he felt was necessary for Tobias' safety and security. He didn't think, nor did he care, about the implications of what that meant for himself in the long-term.

Tobias stirred, then opened his eyes slowly. He looked at Hunter, and for one brief moment, their eyes met. In that instant, it was as though something clicked between the two of them; their unspoken love, their friendship flashed before their eyes. Tobias was no longer Hunter's prisoner; they were best friends again.

Then Tobias spoke.

"Good morning, Hunter."

It wasn't angry like it had been as of late. This was worse, and it made Hunter's heart ache. Tobias sounded sad, defeated, as if all hope had escaped him overnight.

"Toby."

Hunter laid back down and put his head on Tobias' shoulder. "Toby, please. Let me talk."

"I don't really have a choice, do I, Hunt?"

"Of course you have a choice. You could choose to ignore me. But I don't think you will."

Tobias didn't say anything; he closed his eyes again and seemed to be trying to drift back to sleep. Hunter pressed on.

"I love you. I did it because I love you. Please, believe me."

"I do believe you, Hunter," said Tobias quickly. He sounded as though he had expected this. "Believe me. I believe you."

"Then...it's okay. Right?"

"No, Hunter. It is not okay."

Tobias opened his eyes and looked directly into Hunter's dark brown ones. Tobias's eyes—a lighter shade of brown—were so pretty and mesmerizing to Hunter that he found himself lost in them for a moment, until—

"Explain why you did this."

Hunter looked away from the beautiful brown eyes and looked instead up at the ceiling.

"I needed to get you away from Aurora."

"And you thought this was the best way?"

"I think it was the only way."

"Why does everyone think I am so blindly devoted to Aurora?"

At this, Hunter chuckled.

"Because you are, Toby."

"Am not."

"Toby. You have stood up for her on more than one occasion. You watched her strangle your students in front of you. You watched her lose her temper. You heard about how she caused that earthquake. And what did you do?"

Tobias stared at Hunter.

"I…I chose to give her another chance."

"You did. Why?"

"I…well…everyone deserves a second chance, Hunter!"

"By that logic…so do I?"

It was a question; Hunter felt rather silly in asking it, and perhaps that came across to Tobias, for Tobias sighed and said, "Of course you do, Hunter. But you didn't need to cash in on that second chance by kidnapping me."

"If I had just walked up and talked to you—"

"I would have listened. I listened at the hospital, didn't I?"

"I...I suppose that's true. But that was different. You were healing. You weren't ready to fight."

"I tried talking sense into you at Jefferson. I was good and strong then."

Hunter didn't say anything. He just stared at the ceiling for a long while.

"You still haven't answered my question."

"About...?"

"Aurora. Why do you keep giving her second chances?"

Tobias sighed.

"Hunter...I know your experience with her was very different from mine. You weren't there. But Aurora...she was there for me at a time when no one else was. You had just left Bellwater. You didn't tell me anything. You just left. No note, no goodbye, nothing."

"I'm sorry about that."

"Yeah, well, never mind that. One story at a time. Anyway, Aurora found me when I was at my lowest. You see, I tried to drown myself."

21

"You did what now?"

"I tried to drown myself," said Tobias. "You don't understand…you've never been a complete outsider like me. I never had any friends. I never had anyone who really cared about me as a person. My parents were never around, and then they died. I was always moving around, orphanage to orphanage. No one wanted me. No one cared about me. I was just a burden to everyone I was around."

"Then I met you, and everything changed, Hunter. You changed me. You weren't just my best friend. You were my only friend. For so long. And then you left."

The two men didn't say anything; it was simultaneously like nothing had changed between them, and everything had. They would never be the same again.

"After you left, I tried to drown myself. As you know, magic won't let me. I command water. So naturally, I can breathe under it. I went to Bellwater Clearing, that little pond in the middle there. I laid in the bottom of the pool of water for almost a half hour. Of course, I didn't know then, but it became clear to me that drowning just wasn't going to work. So, I used magic to hurl a giant boulder right at my stomach."

"That rock you keep your extra pillow and blanket under?" asked Hunter without thinking, realizing too late that he slipped up.

"Yeah, that's the one. Spying on me, are we?"

"Just a little." Hunter blushed at these words. Luckily, it

was dark in the room, so Tobias couldn't see him.

"Yeah, anyway. Aurora happened to be coming by at the exact moment I flung the boulder at myself. She used her own magic to break it apart and talked me off my ledge. She was there for me, Hunter. She became, in a way, a surrogate for you I suppose."

"What do you mean?"

"Well, she became my only friend for a really long time. Over a year, Hunter. That's a long time to go without talking to your best friend."

"I couldn't."

"Why not?"

"Because..." Hunter hesitated, then said, "Because I didn't want to just be friends."

There was silence between the two men at these words. The sun was starting to rise now; light was filtering in the room quickly. It would soon become very bright, and one of them would need to get up and close the curtains unless they wanted the sunlight in their eyes.

"I love you, Tobias. I want to be with you. I can't just be friends. I want to be more than that. You're my everything. Have me be yours too?"

There was pleading in Hunter's voice at these words.

"Hunter..."

"I wouldn't have done all this stuff if I didn't love you, Tobias! I kidnapped you and I know that was wrong. But you don't understand. The Arcane Rebellion…they ordered me to kill you! And I couldn't! I just couldn't!"

Hunter was now losing control; tears were streaming down his face with every word. It seemed to have cost him everything to let this all out. Tobias turned to face him properly.

"Hunter, listen…"

"I'm sorry, Toby. I'm sorry. You don't deserve this. You deserve so much better."

Tobias continued to try to talk Hunter down, but it was meaningless. Hunter's sobs were echoing around the room. So, Tobias did the only thing he could think of: he pulled Hunter into a giant bear hug.

The two men embraced, lying on a bed together. The magic in the room was such that the sunlight became overpowered; the love these two men felt for each other–though totally different types of love–may have been the strongest thing that had been seen in that cottage, that entire community in decades.

Slowly, Hunter calmed down. He hiccupped, then released himself from Tobias' arms and rolled back over to the side of the bed.

"Hunter. I need you to listen to me very carefully."

Hunter looked at Tobias, his eyes still watery.

Tobias hesitated, then began:

"You can have the best intentions in the world, and still do harm."

Hunter blinked at these words.

"But...but I did it because..."

"Because you love me, yes. I know. I love you too. But you loving me doesn't change the fact that you did me harm. You left me, made me feel abandoned. Then you burned down my school. You attacked my students and colleagues. And to top it all off, you kidnapped me. That doesn't sound like someone who didn't do anything wrong, Hunter. Does it?"

Hunter pondered these words.

"I suppose you're right," he sighed after a few minutes of reflecting on it. "I have acted crazy, haven't I?"

"So, what are you going to do now?" asked Tobias.

"What would you do?"

"If I were you? Well, that depends a great deal. If you truly think the Arcane Rebellion is out to get you..."

"They aren't. I told them I killed you and buried you at Bellwater Clearing."

Tobias blinked in surprise at this.

"Really? That's...a choice, I suppose. Well, since you believe they aren't, I suppose you can't just let me go. But...Hunter, I'm worried. I'm worried about Aurora, and Odion, and everyone else over at Bellwater. What is the Arcane Rebellion going to do to them?"

Hunter hesitated, then said quietly, "We are training your students to kill them."

Tobias opened his mouth in surprise at this.

"What?!"

"Lyra, Elena, and Darian. We teach them magic. They will kill the Bellwater teachers."

"Why would they do that?"

"The twins want revenge on Aurora for trying to strangle Elena. Darian wants revenge on all of you. For ruining his life."

"I saved it..."

"I know, Toby. I know."

"But why would they think we ruined their lives?"

"Well, you said it yourself. Having good intentions doesn't mean you do no harm, or whatever."

Tobias thought about this for a moment.

"I should've let you kill them?"

"We wouldn't have killed them. We were there for them."

"But...what if they didn't go with you?"

"They would've. Just like they went with you."

"You don't know that."

Hunter frowned at this. "I mean, I suppose you're right, but who would want to die rather than come along with us?"

Tobias looked uncomfortable at this question, and Hunter's heart sank.

"C'mon, Toby..."

"You should go."

Tobias turned his back on Hunter, facing the window. Hunter, recognizing the dismissal, got up from the bed and walked towards the door.

"When are you going to decide what you're going to do with me?"

Tobias' question was harsh, and Hunter flinched when he heard the tone with which it was asked.

"I don't know, Tobias. I don't know what I'm going to do with you."

"That wasn't my question. I know you don't know what you'll do. When will you decide?"

"Someday when I stop loving you, I suppose," Hunter answered quietly. Then he turned and left the room.

Chapter Three: Anger & Rage

Hunter teleported to the Arcane Rebellion's secret base: the cruise ship warehouse on the coast. Large cruises didn't typically come out of here, but they did offer some smaller, local cruises on the ocean. He had teleported directly into the warehouse building, where several office workers—used to this—simply greeted him with a friendly, "Hello, Hunter" as he walked through the place. He and Elena had agreed to meet here for training the day before.

Hunter walked through the warehouse, absentmindedly greeting the employees with a curt nod of the head. He wasn't paying much attention until a young man with short, red hair and an earring stopped him.

"Hunter, you have a guest waiting."

It was Bill, the manager of the warehouse. He handled the day-to-day operations of the money laundering scheme of the Arcane Rebellion. The cruises were simply a means to an end for the Rebellion; they needed to make money legally, and Bill had experience on cruise ships. He had grandparents who regularly went on them and had taken him with them on occasion as a child, and he adored them. He didn't use magic, though he knew all about it. He preferred the more mundane ways of doing magic; accounting was his element of choice. Hunter thought that seemed rather boring, though he never mentioned it.

"What's up, Bill?"

"You have a guest waiting in the training room," Bill repeated. "And she's rather...upset. I suggest you don't keep her waiting any longer than is absolutely necessary."

Hunter nodded and continued walking, past Bill, through a locked door leading to the basement of the warehouse. At the bottom of the stairs stood Elena, waiting rather impatiently, tapping her foot as though to get him to move faster.

"Good morning," he greeted her pleasantly.

"Morning," she answered coldly. The two of them walked down the hallway together, not saying a word to each other. There were rooms aligning the hallway; offices, training rooms, classrooms, conference rooms, whatever the Rebellion needed, they had a space for it.

Hunter and Elena entered the room at the end of the hallway. This was a large, empty space designed for practicing spell work. It was also completely soundproof.

"Well, let's get started, shall we?" asked Hunter politely.

In an instant, he shot a blast of fire directly at Elena. She screamed as she was hit by flames—the flames didn't cause any long-term damage (as designed by Hunter) but they did startle her and it still wasn't very comfortable to be hit by them.

"Counterattack. Come on!" shouted Hunter, egging on Elena.

Elena concentrated with all her might, remembering what Aurora and Sabrina had taught her about magic. Then, a small will-o-wisp left the palm of her hand and flew itself directly at Hunter. Hunter put up his hand; a circle seemed to glow around him, protecting him from Elena's feeble attempt at magic. The will-o-wisp hit the center of the circle and went out almost at once.

"You can do better than that!" Hunter yelled again. His left hand held the circle in front of him like a shield; his right hand, meanwhile, gathered flames into a large ball. He flung the ball at Elena; it exploded right in front of her. She flew backwards at the sudden impact and hit the wall of the room, hard. She slid down the wall and gasped in pain, not from the fire, but from the impact of hitting the wall and the blast of the fireball.

Hunter put down his shield, walked over to Elena, and held out his hand. Elena took it, and as soon as she grasped it, she started glowing a yellowish gold just like Hunter's shield; in seconds, she felt as good as she had prior to their little skirmish.

"You need practice," said Hunter candidly.

"Yes, I know," Elena replied shortly; she seemed annoyed.

"Concentrate, Elena. You want revenge on me, don't you? Killing your friends and family? Or how about revenge on dear old Miss Wildwood, for strangling you with a sunflower?"

Elena's face contorted with rage. She screamed and Hunter jumped backwards; her hand had started to become very hot all of a sudden. She screamed again, and punched the air; a fireball, just like the one Hunter had conjured up, flew from her first directly at Hunter. Hunter avoided it only by teleporting away from it just in time; the fireball hit the wall and exploded, hard. The walls shook from the force of the blast. Elena had put her all into the attack.

"So, your anger and rage turned into that attack."

Hunter had reappeared directly behind Elena, frowning.

"While this is progress, don't get complacent, Elena. Anger and rage are great for the short-term, but eventually, those things will subside. You need to channel your emotions into more than just righteous anger. For fire magic to work properly, you need to want it. There needs to be a desire to burn everything standing in your way. Fire is the most destructive of the elemental magics for a reason; to use it properly, you need to have a genuine desire to destroy everything in your path, or it won't work for you the way you want it to."

Elena was looking at him, a mixture of anger and fear on her face. Then he thought more about what he had said, and supposed he saw where she was coming from. He was talking about wanting to burn things down to the ground as though this were a typical thing teachers taught their students. He grinned at her.

"I suppose I am a bit...sociopathic? Psychopathic? I don't know the difference, really."

The two of them spent the next hour or so trading blows back and forth. Hunter had been scorched a few times by Elena, but Hunter purposefully held his magic back so that she wouldn't get hurt. They didn't really speak to each other–beyond Hunter giving words of encouragement here and there–until Elena asked a question.

"Wouldn't it be better to start by teaching me how to block

spells?" asked Elena curiously towards the end of the lesson.

"A lesser mage would think so, yes. But you need to understand that the best defense is a good offense. There won't be a need to block unfriendly spells if you are constantly dishing them out to your opponent. Better to put your opponent in a position where they feel the need to defend themselves rather than attack, as opposed to the alternative."

Shortly after that exchange, the two left the room. They agreed to meet in a couple of days, Hunter giving Elena the task of getting some more practice, then they walked back up to the warehouse and Hunter teleported away from the headquarters.

He reappeared in front of his cottage, where Tobias sat inside. He looked up at it, feeling uneasy. Was he doing the right thing, keeping Tobias here? He couldn't just let him leave; it put himself at risk just as much as it put Tobias in danger. Sabrina and Lucien would undoubtedly find out, and they would put a target on his back just like they did for Tobias. No, he thought to himself. I'm doing the right thing. Just need to keep Tobias safe for as long as I can. Eventually, I'll figure something else out.

He entered the cottage and saw Tobias lying on the floor of the living room. Hunter had chained him up again, with little to no argument from Tobias. Hunter supposed he had little use for his arguments.

"How was school?" asked Tobias mockingly.

"It was a good lesson," replied Hunter smoothly, as though Tobias was his husband and this was a perfectly normal conversation. Tobias glared at him.

"So, have you thought more about when you're going to decide what you're going to do with me?"

"Yes, Tobias. And I still don't know."

"That's not good enough, Hunter!" Tobias roared in frustration. Hunter stared at him. "You need to make a decision, you can't just leave me here!"

Tobias snapped his fingers. Nothing whatsoever happened. Hunter smiled at him sadly.

"Did you forget—"

"No, I most certainly did not forget!" Tobias spat. "When I get out of here, I swear I—"

Hunter ignored the rest of Tobias's threats. He walked upstairs to the little room in the cottage. Perhaps he would take a nap. It had been a long day, after all.

What he hadn't expected was for Tobias to follow him into his room. This surprised Hunter, as Tobias had been chained up. He looked down and saw that Tobias was now so skinny he had been able to slip out of his chains. He would have to rectify that.

"You are not going to ignore me, Hunter Diaz!" Tobias shouted at him. Hunter was rather taken aback by this. It was quite unusual for Tobias to be yelling at him like this. He felt himself getting angry, an emotion he had cautioned Elena against earlier that day.

"What do you want from me, Tobias?!" Hunter roared back.

"To let me go, you buffoon!"

"And where will you go?" asked Hunter scathingly. "You've no one to turn to. You have no magic, and we are in the middle of nowhere."

"Yeah, you saw to that, didn't you, Hunter?!"

Tobias clenched his hand up into a fist and swung at Hunter. Hunter ducked just in time, and headbutted Tobias in the chest. Tobias, weak and frail from lack of nutrition, had the wind knocked out of him. Then Hunter punched him in the face. Tobias hit the floor, hard.

"Idiot!" Hunter roared. "Why would you--?" Then Hunter looked more closely at Tobias. Blood was rushing out of him where Hunter had struck him down. His heart sank.

"Tobias..."

Hunter rushed over to him and knelt beside him. He couldn't believe this. He had lost control of his emotions, done the very thing he had warned Elena against doing. And in the process, he had hurt the man he loved.

"I'm fine, Hunter," Tobias mumbled. His face seemed to be full of blood.

Hunter knelt down to scoop his friend up into a hug, but Tobias pushed him away. "I said, I'm fine!" Tobias snapped. Hunter, recognizing the dismissal, backed away from Tobias. He still eyed him warily just in case there was long-term damage. It seemed Hunter had struck his nose.

"Let me see. Did I break it?"

"No, I don't think so."

With difficulty, Tobias stood up. Hunter extended a hand to try to help him, though Tobias ignored it and stood up on his own volition.

"Let me help you to the bathroom—" Hunter began. Tobias cut him off.

"I can walk, no thanks to you. Leave me alone."

And Tobias left the room, staggering as he walked out. Hunter stared at his back as he left, though he did not follow.

Chapter Four: The Flaw in the Plan

A week had passed since Hunter had his first lesson with Elena. Since then, two more lessons had taken place, and he had to admit he was impressed with how quickly she seemed to be mastering the art of fire; she could now conjure fireballs and sparks in her hand without a second's notice. He thought she would make a formidable opponent one of these days, which might come back to bite him. She still hadn't forgiven him for what he had done at Jefferson High School—a forgiveness that, Hunter thought sadly, he surely didn't deserve anytime soon.

As they wrapped up their last lesson, Hunter felt the need to ask her what her plans were for the rest of the day. It was still rather early, after all. She glared at him, though did not seem so offended that she could ignore the question.

"We—that is to say, Lyra, Darian, and I—have plans."

"Oh? Care to share with the class what kind of plans?"

"Not especially."

This was evidently Elena's idea of polite small talk. Hunter sighed.

"You know, Elena. Giving me these rude, short answers isn't going to bring anyone back."

Elena glared at him. Hunter realized, perhaps too late, that he probably should have thought through what he had said before he actually said it. Oh well, he thought. He had much more pressing matters on his mind at the–

"We are going back to Jefferson."

This startled Hunter to the point of alarm. Apparently, he needed to work on his poker face; Elena looked at him with surprise.

"Is that…does that mean something to you?"

"No, no," Hunter recovered himself quickly. "It just…it just so happens that I have a cottage over there."

"You do? I don't recall ever seeing you there before."

"It was a rather…recent…acquisition of mine."

"I see," Elena replied sharply. "So, you kill our families and friends and you take their homes too?"

Hunter thought this conversation should have ended ten minutes ago but said nothing in response. Elena, glaring at him, left the room. Hunter's mind continued racing; he needed to make sure Elena, Lyra, and Darian saw nothing whatsoever resembling Tobias. For his own sake. And more importantly, for Tobias's. He knew he could take on the children, even three on one, but he could not count on them not running to Sabrina or Lucien about this if they found out. From what he heard and had picked up on from Elena, their lessons with Lucien and Sabrina were going quite well.

Hunter left the cruise ship port and teleported home. Walking up the steps into the cottage, he found Tobias in his usual spot in the middle of the living room floor. Hunter sighed. The man was filthy; he had refused to bathe since Hunter had brought him here. Hunter had tried every plea, bribe, and threat he could muster, but Tobias wasn't budging. Tobias got like this sometimes, where he refused to take care of himself. Hunter didn't mind, though his nostrils thought Tobias could do with a bar of soap.

"Good afternoon," said Hunter cheerfully. Tobias glanced up at him.

"Did you decide–?"

"No," Hunter retorted shortly. Then he walked right past Tobias and into the kitchen, preparing to fix himself and Tobias a snack. He brought cheese and crackers on two small plates into the living room, the poor man's charcuterie board as he liked to call it. His absolute favorite.

Tobias looked up at him again as he entered the living room for a second time.

"You've never walked by me like that," Tobias said curiously.

"What?" asked Hunter absentmindedly, his mind still on his conversation with Elena.

"You ignored me when I began to ask my question."

"Because you ask the same question every day, Toby."

Tobias shook his head. "Something's bothering you. Spit it out."

Hunter sighed, recognizing defeat. Tobias knew him too well to be fooled by his attempts at deflection.

"Elena, her sister, and her boyfriend are coming to Jefferson."

Tobias stared at him.

"You...invited them here?"

"No, they're coming back home seemingly unannounced."

"Why?"

"No idea. But we need to keep you away from their prying eyes."

"Do they know you live out here?"

"I...I told Elena I do, yes."

"Why would you do that?"

Hunter looked sheepishly down at the floor of the living room. "I didn't...mean to, exactly. It just kind of happened. When she told me she was coming here, she caught me off guard and noticed something was up. So, I told her. She knew there was something weird going on."

Tobias chuckled. Hunter's ears perked up; it was like music to him. "Hunter, you think you're so...hardcore but you're really just a teddy bear."

Hunter was somewhat offended by this, but the tone in Tobias's voice was the most pleasant it had been all week. He smiled at his friend.

"I'm glad you think so. She does not."

"Well, yeah. You did kill her entire family and friends."

"You know, why does everyone keep bringing that up?"

"It's…kind of a big deal, Hunter."

At this, they both laughed a little bit. They knew they probably shouldn't be laughing at it, and yet they were anyway. After thirty seconds or so, they just grinned at each other.

"Are you going to tell me why you attacked them in the first place now?"

Hunter's grin faded, though not out of shock or alarm; more out of curiosity.

"I mean, Sabrina and Lucien told us we need to drive up recruitment," he answered slowly. "We…that is to say, Ted and I…talked it over and he mentioned this place in Jefferson. I told him about how the two of us used to go and teach in high schools to recruit for Bellwater. He thought that would take too long. So we just…burned the school to the ground. And whoever survived the longest, we would offer to let them leave with us."

"And that doesn't seem…harsh?"

"Well, when you put it that way, I can see where someone would find it…harsh, I suppose."

The two sat in silence for a little while after that. Hunter was lost in thought. He still wondered if he was doing the right thing, keeping Tobias here against his will. He thought back to what Tobias had told him before. "You can have the best intentions, and still do harm." He thought he could see, dimly, what Tobias had meant at these words, though it did little to comfort him.

Did I do more harm than good, in trying to protect him?

Hunter pondered the possibility of letting Tobias go. Unfortunately, however, it was far too late for them to go down that road. For one thing, Tobias was too weak from the magic draining chains and enchantments Hunter himself had put around his cottage. He wouldn't be able to use magic for a while. Letting him go on foot wouldn't get him very far, especially considering they were currently in a community where Tobias was presumed dead. Questions would be raised, and it would not go unnoticed that a man presumed dead for several weeks since the time of the Jefferson fire was now up and walking around the neighborhood. That would possibly cause panic and pandemonium. No, it would draw far too much attention. Hunter considered bringing him back to Bellwater Cottage, but Sabrina and Lucien kept close tabs on the place; it would be impossible to bring him back to Aurora or Odion or anyone else in the Bellwater Mages group without immediately alerting them. And if Sabrina or Lucien found out about what he was up to, he would be next on the chopping block for destruction.

The truth was, Hunter was far more concerned for Tobias's safety than his own. He was scared. He knew Tobias trusted Aurora, but there was something about her that just seemed off to him. He also didn't fully trust Sabrina or Lucien, despite his working for the Rebellion. Him working for them was more of a means to an end than anything else. He knew he didn't really have a right to be; Tobias was more than capable of holding his own against enemy mages, and had even managed to best Hunter on more than one occasion. But he couldn't help feeling protective of the man.

Hunter had never felt this way about any other person besides Tobias. Upon finding out that he was gay–something that Hunter had not been afraid to admit from a young age–he had been relentlessly bullied and teased at school for his sexual orientation. Even his parents, whom he no longer had a relationship with, had taken a firm stance against his homosexuality from the beginning. His father had gone so far as to beat him with a baseball bat–Hunter had been an avid baseball player in his youth–upon finding out he was gay. Shortly thereafter, Hunter ran away from home and joined in with a small gang in Mexico. Not one of the larger gangs, mind you, but a small gang composed mostly of youth. While in the gang, he had committed several minor crimes including shoplifting, vandalism, and trespass–nothing out of the ordinary for a teenage kid, he supposed, but upon coming to the United States on a legal visa in high school, he had initially gotten lots of racist looks and comments from several people. He had moved with a foster family to Bellwater. Where he had attended Bellwater Academy. There is where he met–

"Hunter?"

Tobias was asking him a question. Hunter jumped and looked around.

"What is it?"

"I asked you if you would mind if I showered?"

Hunter stared at Tobias.

"Bathing again, are we?"

Tobias shrugged. "You're going to do what you're going to do, Hunter. You've shown me, deep down, you're still a good guy."

Chapter Five: Progress

Elena was gasping for breath. She had just been through a particularly brutal scrimmage with Hunter; he was standing over her like a hawk, waiting for a sign of trouble. She made eye contact with him.

"So, how was going back to your old high school last night?" he asked casually.

"We...we didn't stick around for long. It was too hard...emotionally," she managed to let out between gasps. "I just need...another minute..."

Hunter turned around and faced the wall, away from Elena. He was relieved that the children had supposedly found it too difficult to follow through with a long visit to their old high school neighborhood; it would make hiding Tobias much easier.

"Where do you live though, Hunter? Maybe we could stop by sometime?"

Hunter turned and glared at Elena. "And why would you want to do that?"

Elena shrugged. "Beats the hell out of coming all the way here for training, doesn't it?"

"I don't mind it," he said quickly. Elena looked at him, suspiciously.

"Why don't you want me to know where you live?" she asked him cautiously.

"Because it's none of your business," he snapped. "You shouldn't be visiting me anyway; it's improper. I'm your teacher, and a lot older than you–"

"But you can burn down our schools and kill everyone we love? Maybe your sense of morality should get checked out."

Hunter opened his mouth to retort when a woman's voice said from behind him, "Miss Wilkins has a point, you know, Hunter."

He turned and saw Sabrina Braithwaite approaching him, with a wide smile on her face. She was wearing her usual long, red gown and carrying a bright red handbag, as though she were going to a formal dinner party. Behind her was Lucien Rodson, his large belly hanging out of his t-shirt slightly. Elena's sister, Lyra, and her boyfriend Darian were also behind the Rebellion leadership. They nodded to Elena, then glared at Hunter.

"Sabrina! Lucien! To what do I owe the pleasure?"

"We thought it'd be neat to have all six of us meet for a few classes," Lucien responded kindly. "Learn from each other, kind of thing. What do you think, Hunter?"

Hunter thought this was a terrible idea, for several reasons. "That sounds like a great idea!" he replied politely.

"Excellent," said Sabrina soothingly. "Why don't you let me start things off then, Hunter? Ladies first and all." She pulled herself up to her full height. "I am working with Darian on the nuances of Earth magic," she reminded everyone. "Lucien is working with Lyra on lightning magic—or the use of the letter 'L', whichever is higher priority to them, I suppose." She chuckled at her little joke. Hunter held back a snort, with difficulty, not because the joke was funny. "Hunter and Elena, meanwhile, are working through fire magic."

"Darian, stand across from me. There ya go…and go ahead and use magic to try to knock me off my feet. Everyone else, make sure you're far enough away to not get hit but not so far you can't see what's going on."

Darian nodded, then walked over to stand where Sabrina had indicated. He looked at the ground and concentrated hard. He seemed to be having a tough time; he had stretched out his hands and had his palms facing the ground, but nothing seemed to be happening. The class waited for a minute or two, before Sabrina said, "Remember, Darian, to use magic, you need to use your emotions. They are a tool—boys often have a hard time using their emotions as a tool, often preferring to bottle them up instead. You need to—"

A faint tremor seemed to happen between Darian and Sabrina. Sabrina didn't fall down, but she did seem to be startled a bit. She smiled at him.

"There you go! Now, try this."

She reached into her handbag and pulled out a small packet of what looked like seeds. "These are tulip seeds," she said. "See if you can grow them. You need to feel connected and loved to be able to use magic effectively, remember."

Darian took the seeds from her, then pulled one into his

47

hand. He closed his eyes and rubbed his finger on top of the seed. It quickly sprouted into a small flower; it didn't seem to be completely developed yet, but was certainly something a novice gardener would have been proud of. Sabrina smiled at him again.

"Nice job, my boy!"

Darian smiled at her as she patted him on the back proudly. "Now, Lyra, Lucien. Why don't you show us what you've been up to?"

Lyra and Lucien walked over to where Darian and Sabrina had been, facing each other.

"Remember, Lyra. To control lightning means to control the weather itself. It's not an easy element to command."

"I know," she said dryly. She stood and surveyed Lucien carefully. Then she stretched out a hand and pointed a finger at the light fixture hanging overhead. The light fixture seemed to fizzle, then burn out. Lucien smiled at her.

"Very good, Lyra! Now, can you turn it back on?"

Lyra took considerably more time to turn it back on than to get it to turn off; she seemed to be struggling with it. After a few minutes, Lucien reminded her, "To use magic is to control your feelings and emotions. Let them run through you, let the magic of your emotions be the magic you need."

The light seemed to flicker a little bit, then eventually turned back on, though significantly dimmer than before. Lucien smiled at her.

"That's progress, Miss Lyra!"

Lyra seemed a little sad, but also took the compliment and didn't say anything in response. Hunter and Elena moved to stand where Lucien and Lyra had been moments ago.

"Alright, Elena. Moment of truth. Can you do it? Can you command fire?"

Hunter knew the answer to this, of course, and had luckily blocked the ball of fire that had come soaring towards him just in the nick of time. Lyra and Darian screamed. He glanced at Sabrina and Lucien, who both seemed surprised and–was it angry?

Elena threw another ball of fire at Hunter. He blocked it with a lazy flick of his wrist. Then Elena twisted her arm in midair, and fire–seemingly out of nowhere–appeared and twisted itself into the shape of a small dinosaur. The dino-fire charged at Hunter. Hunter hadn't expected this; he had never taught her how to do this specifically, though supposedly she could have used context clues to figure out how to make something like this work. He snapped his fingers, and the dinosaur vanished into a puff of smoke.

"I think that's enough!"

Hunter and Elena both turned to see Sabrina, fuming. Darian and Lyra were looking at Elena in fear, as though she had grown two more heads. Sabrina and Lucien were glaring at Hunter.

"Children," said Lucien soothingly. "Would you please excuse us for a–"

"I want to work with Hunter," said Lyra sharply.

"Me too," said Darian.

Sabrina and Lucien didn't seem surprised by this, but also didn't seem happy about it.

"We will...discuss rotating out. You are all excused. Report to us on Tuesday for your next lessons."

Lyra, Elena, and Darian were rather grumpy but left the training room. Lucien turned to Hunter.

"What the hell do you think you're doing?!"

"Teaching," Hunter retorted. "What are you two doing, babysitting?"

"She...she shouldn't be able to do that at this point!"

Hunter sighed. "I don't know about Darian and Lyra, but Elena...she seems particularly pissed about what Aurora Wildwood did to her. She can't control it. Her emotions, as you both say, are manifesting themselves in ways she cannot control. That's probably, at least in part, why her magic is so much stronger than the other two."

"Dear," Sabrina interjected; it looked like Lucien was about to interrupt. "Hunter is right. Besides, we instructed him to make sure Elena was ready for combat. Perhaps the two of us should look at our teaching methods and expedite things a bit?"

Lucien closed his mouth and didn't speak. Sabrina turned back to Hunter.

"The issue isn't how capable Elena is," Sabrina said calmly. "It's how incapable Lyra and Darian are. Perhaps we are not as effective teachers as you, Hunter. I think there may be something to the idea that you take on teaching all three students magic."

Hunter gaped at her. "But…what will you two do?"

"Leadership duties, administrative tasks. That sort of thing, you know. We both still teach at Bellwater Academy as well. You have much more time than we do to devote to teaching."

Hunter supposed they had a point, though he wasn't happy about it. "Do I have a choice?" he grunted.

"Of course you do," said Sabrina sweetly. "You could just walk out of here and leave. But you won't, will you? Because you know we're your only friends!"

Sabrina turned away from him, Lucien following in her stead. Hunter looked after them, feeling like this was their intention all along, somehow.

Chapter Six: The Delinquent Duo

Aurora Wildwood, newly named Principal of Bellwater Academy, was walking down the hallway. She was wearing a fine suit with her long, black hair curled up for the day. As she walked down the hallway, students quickly stopped their idle chatter; no one wanted to get on the bad side of Miss Wildwood.

Aurora, however, paid them no mind. She had a destination set in her mind, and she was racing to her math teacher's classroom as quickly as she dared, for she didn't want to attract any unwanted attention. It didn't take her long to reach the classroom; she knocked and entered quietly.

Alone in the room was a well-dressed young man grading papers: Odion Montgomery.

"No, Allison, I haven't finished grading your–oh, Miss Wildwood. Forgive me."

"No forgiveness needed, Mr. Montgomery."

There was a certain amount of tension between the two adults. Aurora refused to meet Odion's eyes, he noticed.

"How can I help you?"

"We need to meet."

"A teacher's union meeting?" asked Odion, surprised; Sabrina, as acting leader of the Bellwater Mages, was normally the one who called for the teacher's union meetings—which were really meetings between the Bellwater Mages.

"Not exactly. No. I want to meet just the two of us."

"Why?" asked Odion, suspiciously.

"Because…because I'm worried, Odion. Tobias has disappeared before, but not like this. He was severely weakened by that gunshot by my predecessor. I really don't think he would just up and disappear like this unless…unless something happened to him."

Aurora was practically in tears at this. Odion could tell she was upset. He shifted uncomfortably; he had no faith in Aurora, though he couldn't pretend like he wasn't concerned about Tobias.

"What are you suggesting, Aurora?"

It was the use of her first name that caused her to look at him.

"We—you and I—need to go and find him."

"Why us?"

"Because I think we have been infiltrated."

"And what gives you that idea?"

Aurora turned around to make sure the door was locked;

it was. Then she waved her hand at the door, and the windows; the cracks were instantly covered in what looked like red roses. At first glance these could easily pass for wall decorations or window clings, but Odion knew these were the real deal. Aurora had used magic to seal his classroom from any potential eavesdroppers. Odion frowned at this.

"You just used magic at school."

"I'm aware, but the cottage isn't safe now. Not with Sabrina and Lucien hanging around there all the time. We need to talk here."

She was talking quickly, and her words connected with Odion as he realized the severity of the situation.

"Have you been practicing your magic like I told you to do?"

"Yes, ma'am."

"Good. We need to find Hunter Diaz."

Odion sighed. "I know Foxton said that he saw Tobias being carried off by Hunter, but I can't find any trace of either of them, Aurora. Everyone's looking."

"No, they're not. Sabrina and Lucien are playing it off like this is nothing out of the ordinary. All they care about now is recruiting more members."

Odion frowned.

"They're not continuing the search?"

"No, they say that because Tobias has done this before, that he'll inevitably show up. They insist Foxton must have been mistaken by what he saw in all the fighting."

"You don't believe that, do you, Aurora?"

"Of course not," she snapped, then quickly said calmly, "No, I think they're trying to distract us from their true mission. But Agatha is still out of sorts with her broken hip, and Matilda is—well, she's unreliable, if nothing else. I know you're new to magic, but I need you to do this with me, Odion."

"What about our jobs?"

Aurora sighed, then said, "I have arranged for Reginald Quirk to come in and take over for you for the time being."

"Reginald? That old coot who lets the students do whatever they want while he sits and solves crossword puzzles all day? You think he can teach math in my absence?"

"He used to, a long time ago. He's not as young as he used to be, but I think he'll manage for the time being. I told him this was a temporary assignment."

"Do you have any idea where to start?"

"I do, actually," Aurora replied, pulling out a small photograph from her suit pocket. The picture was of a short, chubby middle-aged man who seemed vaguely familiar to Odion. "In the files you and Tobias recovered from the cruise warehouse, I found this picture. His name is Ted. He's the one who burned down Jefferson High with Hunter. It says in those files that

55

Hunter inherited a plot of land from someone Ted knew from Jefferson. Unfortunately, the file didn't say where exactly this plot of land was. Undoubtedly, the Arcane Rebellion is using that land to house their own members. We will track down Ted and find out the truth from him on Hunter's whereabouts."

"And what will you do?"

"I'm coming with you, but I can't stay the whole time. My absence will not go unnoticed. I have arranged for a minor surgery next week. I will be gone the whole week from school. Sabrina and Lucien know, of course. They don't suspect a thing."

"For now," said Odion gravely.

"For now," Aurora agreed. She turned and began walking out of the room, calling as she went, "we leave Friday after school. Be ready. We'll be driving; he only lives about four hours away."

The next few days went by very slowly for Odion and Aurora. Each of them was ecstatic about finally having a mission, but as what tends to happen when one is eager for something to happen, time has a way of moving seemingly slower than is possible. Aurora had a hard time making sure that Sabrina and Lucien were unaware of their plan; she couldn't be sure, but she also didn't see how they would have found out about it. Neither of the magical leaders questioned her or Odion about their conversation at Bellwater Academy, nor were they acting funny or suspiciously about anything.

Aurora had another concern: Foxton Gray. Foxton had witnessed Tobias being kidnapped by Hunter and was arguably at fault for the whole incident occurring in the first place. The foolish boy had tracked down his old teacher and asked him to hunt down the Arcane Rebellion members who had killed his family and friends—a noble desire, Aurora thought bitterly, but one that Tobias never would have agreed to, and one that likely allowed Hunter to move in and kidnap Tobias. Tobias' greatest weakness—as well as his greatest strength—was his ability to love and protect others. Aurora knew he had sacrificed himself to save the boy. She just wasn't sure it was worth it.

Foxton was now beginning to act out in class, refusing to do his homework, suffering academically. He was popping up all over the place in Aurora's office; it seemed he was trying to find reasons to be sent to her office just for an excuse to ask her about the search for Tobias. Aurora wasn't foolish enough to tell him anything, and she told him point-blank that next time he was sent to her office, she would be left with no choice but to suspend him. Unfortunately, that time had come: Foxton had been sent to her office by Sabrina for refusing to stop talking to Finnian Cleary—his best friend—about Tobias. Aurora was furious at this, and true to her word, she suspended Foxton for three days. She also told him that if he talked about such things at school again, the consequences would be much more severe than a mere suspension.

Finally, Friday afternoon came, and Aurora met Odion at his apartment in downtown Bellwater. However, he wasn't the only one at the apartment; a pale, ginger-haired boy with freckles answered the door when Aurora knocked, and she looked startled.

"Foxton?"

"Hello, Miss Wildwood," he said, sounding annoyed.

"What are you doing here?"

"I live here, remember? This is my 'safe house' that you assigned me." She could tell from his tone that he didn't think much of her making house calls; it was clear he was annoyed that she suspended him. However, he perked up as he realized something. "You're here for Odion, aren't you?"

"Naturally. Did you think I was here for you?"

Foxton frowned. "You could've at least pretended, ya know." He turned and shouted, "Odion! Aurora's here!"

Odion came up behind Foxton just then, a large backpack on his back. It was odd to see him in jeans and a hooded sweatshirt; he was normally dressed up.

"You didn't need to shout, Foxton. The apartment isn't that large."

"Yeah, well. I felt like it." He glanced at Aurora, then returned his gaze to Odion, glaring.

"No need to cop an attitude, mister," said Odion, sternly. "Don't forget, since you've been suspended, I've given you a list of chores. I expect them to be done by the time we get back."

"Yes, master," Foxton replied sarcastically. Odion scowled.

"And there's no need for that. Oh, and no friends over. I don't need Taylor or Andy or anyone trashing up the place."

"No need to worry about that. Finnian isn't about to trash

anything up."

"What about the other guys you talk to?"

"I don't give a damn about any of them." Foxton sighed, then said, "You guys should just go."

"You have my number if anything comes up."

Foxton nodded, then slammed the door in Odion's face.

"Rude," Odion grumbled but didn't say anything more on the subject. The duo left the apartment and walked out to Aurora's car. She was driving a Ford Focus; nothing too crazy or fancy, but reliable and easy to blend into a crowd of people if necessary.

"So how far away is Ted, do you think?" asked Odion. He seemed eager, excited; it felt good to have a mission again.

"The Rebellion's records indicate he lives about two hours south of here."

"We're going to his house?" asked Odion, surprised. "That seems...forward? Dangerous?"

"Do you have a better idea?"

"I suppose not."

"Well, if you can think of something in the next two hours, we can discuss. But realistically, confronting him at his house is probably the most sure-fire way to get him to talk."

"Or the most sure-fire way to get us killed."

"We'll be doing the killing, if necessary, Odion. I studied this man. He specializes in fire magic. He's not particularly powerful; we just need to confront him two on one."

"Sounds like you have this all figured out," muttered Odion under his breath as Aurora began to drive.

Two and a half hours non-stop and they had finally reached their destination: a little town south of Bellwater where the man called Ted was supposed to reside, according to documents seized by Tobias and Odion from the Arcane Rebellion several weeks beforehand. Odion, who had been lazily dozing in the passenger seat of the car, awoke with a start and looked around at his surroundings.

It truly was a small quaint town, like Bellwater. There weren't many buildings around; it seemed there was a post office, a bar, and a couple of houses. Odion supposed one of these must belong to Ted.

"What's our plan?"

Aurora got out of the car and walked up to a light post. She hugged it; Odion was very confused. Then he realized what she was doing: she was scrying.

"I don't see anyone resembling his description anywhere near here," Aurora sighed. "But it seems foolish not to ask in the bar anyway."

The two of them entered the bar, Odion in his jeans and hoodie and Aurora in her business dress suit from school that day. The bar was mostly empty; the bartender–an old man who was wiping a mug with a towel that looked like it had seen better days–stood behind the bar and nodded at them when they entered. There was one person sitting at the bar, a young man who looked like he had just turned twenty-one. And sitting at a table in the back of the bar, was a young woman who looked like she had vivid blue hair tucked in a beanie. She was shrouded in shadow, and neither Aurora nor Odion could make any of her features out.

Aurora walked right up to the bartender and sat down at the bar, as far away from the young man as possible. Odion stood beside her, looking around casually.

"What can I get you?" asked the bartender, not unkindly, though not overly friendly either.

"Information," said Aurora in an undertone. "On a man called Ted."

"Ted?" the bartender replied. "He hasn't been in here in…gee, two or three months? I think he moved."

"Any idea where we can find him?"

"Who's asking?"

"A friend. I just need to talk to him."

"He's never had 'friends' come here asking about him before."

The bartender was inconveniently sharp and protective of his patrons, it seemed to Aurora. She sighed.

"I have an inheritance for him. From his recently deceased mother."

The bartender stared at her.

"I...see. Well, I'm afraid he's not around here anymore. Moved away, I'm not sure where he went off to. But he's not here anymore."

Aurora sighed. "Thank you for your time."

The two of them turned to leave.

"If Ted comes back here," the bartender called after them, which made Aurora and Odion flinch, "who should I say was asking?"

At this, Aurora turned around and walked back towards the bar, pulling from her pocket a small badge that looked like it belonged to a police detective.

"Oh, sorry. I didn't show you my badge. I'm with the police."

The bartender inspected it.

"Ah, that makes much more sense," he said, with a sigh of relief. "Okay, I'll let him know to call the station if he ever does make it back here."

Aurora turned to leave, Odion holding the door for her. The two of them walked back to the car and got in, Aurora slamming the door in frustration.

"What a waste of a trip. Come on. Let's get back, I suppose."

"What's our next move?"

However, Aurora had barely had time to start the car and put it into drive when water came crashing down onto the car; it pummeled the car with such force that the windows shattered and the roof fell on top of them. Neither Aurora nor Odion saw it coming, but they quickly teleported out of the car and onto the sidewalk next to the car. They looked around, and Odion pointed at a small figure on top of the bar.

It was the girl with long, vivid blue hair who was sitting in the bar; it seemed she had caused the sudden burst of water to appear from nothing and crash on top of their car. She noticed they had left the car and waved her hands in front of her. Instantly, a jet of water soared through the air and narrowly avoided hitting Odion in the face. He jumped out of the way at the last second and the water instead hit a tree nearby. The tree was uprooted from the force of the water and went soaring through the air, out of sight.

The woman waved her hands again, casting spells so frequently neither Aurora nor Odion had a chance to respond to the magic. A tidal wave of water–seemingly out of nothing–soared up from behind the bar. Odion gasped, and Aurora teleported away out of sight.

The tidal wave crashed and covered everything in sight, completely submerging the street with water. Odion gasped and held his breath, closing his eyes as he did so. He felt the water completely fill up the street; soon, he was covered head to toe in water.

He opened his eyes and took a breath, and discovered to his astonishment that he could breathe! It was just as easy as breathing air would be. He looked around and realized that the girl had completely flooded the street with water. It was like they were at the bottom of a lake, as though a tsunami had come in and swept through the ground. There didn't seem to be any damage done to the buildings or cars or anything, but they were most certainly underwater. For a split second, Odion wondered why he was still breathing. Then he remembered something Tobias had told him several weeks ago:

"They're resistant to their own branch of magic. You can try and drown me in water all you want, but it won't work. I can breathe underwater."

Odion realized, I specialize in water magic, so this doesn't bother me at all.

Odion!

Aurora?

Distract her! I can't fight underwater!

Odion looked around. The street was covered in water; they were completely submerged. It was as though they were at the bottom of a lake. It was the most surreal thing Odion had ever experienced.

"You specialize in water magic?"

He turned around and looked; the young woman was

standing mere feet from him, eyeing him up closely. She, too, could speak and breathe underwater.

"I thought for sure you'd drown, like your friend. Interesting. I've never met anyone who specializes in water magic other than me. The Rebellion seems to frown on it."

"Really?" asked Odion, thinking fast. "Why's that?"

"Dunno," the girl replied, sounding bored. "But you won't find out."

She waved her hand again. Instantly, a giant whirlpool started to form around Odion. It pulled him in, and he started spinning, around and around. The spinning made him a bit dizzy, though the water nor the whirlpool itself seemed to have no effect on him. He felt like he was on a tilt a whirl, a carnival ride he used to really enjoy as a kid. Aside from the dizziness, this was something he seemed to be *enjoying.*

I need to get out of here, he thought to himself after spinning for a little bit. He remembered a trick Agatha had taught him about water magic and decided to try it out.

He put his hands out in front of himself and concentrated as hard as he could considering he was being tossed around in a whirlpool. After a few seconds, his body started to spin, in the opposite direction of the whirlpool. He spun faster and faster, until eventually the whirlpool subsided.

The girl looked impressed at this.

"I didn't know you could do that!" she sounded amazed.

Odion decided to use this as an opportunity to launch a surprise attack on her. He jetted towards her with the speed of a gushing geyser. He tackled her head-on. She hadn't been expecting it and went soaring through the water high into the air. Odion lost sight of her for a moment, so he again propelled himself forward until he too reached the surface of the water.

Odion's head emerged from the water. The first thing he saw was a cascade of roses flying through the water right towards the girl. Odion noticed these roses had thorns on their stems that looked like they had been sharpened by a professional. The girl was pummeled by the roses, and she screamed in surprise and agony. The rose petals themselves explode upon contact, or so it seemed; there were several small "bangs" once the roses hit their mark. For what seemed like minutes, the girl was floating in midair being attacked by exploding roses and their sword-like thorns. Odion didn't notice the water was retreating quickly, being sucked back into the ground or the air; he was breathing oxygen again instead of water, and he was now standing firmly on the ground.

Aurora appeared alongside him once the water had finished. Odion looked around; it was as though nothing had happened at all other than the tree that the girl had hit with her water blast was still gone.

"Come on, we need to go," said Aurora quickly. Odion turned to look at the girl; she was unconscious. He heard Aurora snap her fingers, and a long, thick vine appeared in her hand. She whipped it at the girl–who was still flying in a whirlwind of roses– and the vine wrapped itself around her, tightly, covering her head to toe. Aurora made a sudden hand gesture, and the girl slammed into the ground before being dragged over to Aurora and Odion. She was unconscious, and–from what Odion could tell–barely alive.

"Nice work, Odion," said Aurora quickly, making sure her prisoner was tightly held in the confines of the vine, "now let's get out of here. Let's teleport. To...to," she seemed to be struggling to come up with a place to teleport to.

"Bellwater Clearing?"

"Too dangerous. Sabrina has had eyes on that place like a hawk."

"What about your office at Bellwater Academy?"

"No, I don't think that will work...but that gives me an idea."

Chapter Seven: An Unexpected House Call

Tobias had no idea how long he had been in Hunter's…house, he supposed. The four walls surrounding him and keeping him prisoner seemed to be more of a jail cell than anything, but he supposed a jail would be slightly less comfortable. At least he was usually by himself. Hunter was so busy with the Arcane Rebellion that he had hardly been here for the last several…days? Weeks? Tobias had no idea. He knew that when he first arrived, leaves were falling and cluttering the ground with pretty colors. Now, a thin layer of snow was on the ground covering it up in a white blanket.

Tobias sighed and looked away from the window, into the confines of his space. Loneliness and powerlessness were the first words to come to mind for Tobias when he thought about this space. The only company he had was his captor: Hunter Diaz. His best friend. Or so he thought. At first, Tobias had refused to so much as look at him. He had refused baths, showers, meals, changes of clothes, everything the man had offered him. Hunter had begrudgingly accepted Tobias' refusal, but Tobias was no fool; Hunter was ticked off that he couldn't get Tobias to eat or bathe. This wasn't so far out of the ordinary, as Hunter knew, even on a good day. But based on Hunter's reactions to Tobias, he guessed that it had been quite a while since he had been brought here.

At first, Tobias had put a lot of thought and effort into escaping his prison. But it was no use. Hunter had him held in chains that were deadbolted to the wall of the living room. These chains were enchanted to prevent him from using magic to fight Hunter or try to escape–something Hunter had been quick to remind him of. While he had been dragged unconscious to this house by his former friend, Hunter had made sure to securely fasten him to the wall and drain his energy. This prevented Tobias from making an escape or attempting to use magic. He couldn't teleport, he couldn't scry, he couldn't even telepathically communicate with the other mages from Bellwater. Not that he could anyway, if he was being honest with himself. He had never been very good at that.

Nowadays, Tobias seemed a lot more content to just sit around and…wait to die. Perhaps he shouldn't feel this way, and he didn't want to feel so depressed. But it was easier than trying to fight back against his master, Hunter. Tobias shook his head in frustration; he shouldn't be thinking of Hunter like that. For all of Hunter's faults, he still had some good in him. He had seen that just the other day, when he had finally agreed to bathe. And it was a good thing he had; he had been filthy.

Tobias turned his attention instead to the Bellwater Mages. Aurora Wildwood, their fearless, badass leader. She would undoubtedly be looking for him by now, she usually did when he disappeared like this even though no one else really believed her. She usually had something of an anger management problem, and he shuddered to think what would become of Hunter if Aurora got ahold of him somehow. Then there was Odion Montgomery, a new recruit to Bellwater. Young and well-dressed, Odion was the most immature man he had ever met. This wasn't an insult; on the contrary, Tobias adored this about Odion. But he had to admit that Odion would not be very helpful when it comes to magical prowess. He also thought about Foxton Gray. A young boy with red hair and freckles, Foxton had an air of kindness to him that was contagious to all who knew him. Tobias had allowed himself to be captured by Hunter to save Foxton, and he had succeeded in that endeavor at the very least. He also considered Finnian Cleary, Foxton's best friend who had been shy, reserved, and timid. He knew not what the status of Finnian was, but he was sure both boys were being kept safe by the Bellwater Mages. There was also Agatha O'Connor, who had just broken her hip. Powerful, fearless and not one to take shit from anyone, Agatha would be a strong person to have on your side in a fight. Matilda Carrington was another mage, relatively inexperienced, though well-meaning Tobias was sure. He didn't really know her all that well. Then of course, there was Sabrina Braithwaite and Lucien Rodson: the moles, the spies for the Arcane Rebellion.

He often found himself wondering about Aurora, and Odion, and the others over at Bellwater. What were they doing? Were they looking for him? Was it possible they had forgotten about him? He had had thoughts like this before, of course, but he felt he had never been this isolated for this long. Granted, he had no idea how long it had really been, but he digressed. He supposed time seemed to move more slowly when you were being held captive. Time itself was not something you could use magic to impact directly, after all.

Tobias sighed. There was no clock in the house, and Hunter had destroyed his cell phone when he had kidnapped him. He never left Tobias with a cell phone; that would be silly of Hunter to do when he had worked so hard to—

Tobias stopped and listened hard as he heard...could it be? Footsteps? And not just one set of them either. He looked back out the window, and for good measure, hid behind the couch. An ideal place to see but not be seen from the window. If this was somehow Bellwater Mages, Tobias would of course show himself; but he couldn't be sure that they weren't Arcane

Rebellion spellcasters instead. If they were, not only would they kill Tobias, but they would also undoubtedly track down and kill Hunter for treason as well. Perhaps Tobias shouldn't care so much about that, but he did anyway; that was just the type of person Tobias was.

"He SAID he lives around here, Lyra! This is the only house we haven't investigated yet. Don't you want to check it out?"

Tobias was shocked; it was Elena Wilkins, one of the students he had saved from burning alive in the fire that had consumed this very community. And she supposedly was talking to her sister, Lyra.

"When the three 'masters' sent us out of there so they could talk, I hardly think they meant to go barge into random houses where we used to live, Elena," Lyra's voice, her twin sisters, could be heard over the muffled sounds of footsteps on snow. Tobias was only able to hear because Hunter had bewitched the house to be unnaturally quiet, to hear potential intruders as soon as possible.

"Yes, well, Hunter said he lives around here supposedly. I still think it's worth checking out, if we're going to get revenge on them?"

"Revenge?" a boy's voice, and Tobias recognized Darian Keen, the boy whom he had resurrected and brought back to life mere weeks–months? ago. "Who said anything about revenge, Elena?"

"I did, Darian. If you don't have the balls to–"

"Lovebirds," Lyra sang. "Save the fighting for another day, preferably one when we aren't trespassing onto private property."

"Who cares if we're trespassing? They killed all the police anyway."

Tobias thought there was too much truth in those words for either her sister or her boyfriend to argue with her, between Hunter and Aurora's actions in the last few weeks, and the teenagers seemed to agree. Tobias heard the trio approach the window and he quickly ducked behind the couch, listening hard.

The good thing about this time of year was that it was already starting to get dark out. Tobias never lit any lights at night, so the interior of the house was already quite obscure from the outside looking in. This would make it much harder for the teenagers to see what was going on in the house. His biggest concern was the wall of chains that Tobias was still attached to. Hunter had allowed him to be attached only at the leg, so he could move around as he pleased now, but it would still be difficult hiding a giant chain from the teenagers if they knew what to look for.

He knew instinctively that the trio were looking into the house, inspecting it. He held his breath as he listened hard.

"I don't see anything, Elena." Darian's voice.

"I don't either." He assumed this was Lyra's voice, though they being twins it was hard to tell for sure.

"Me neither," he heard the other twin admit. "I thought maybe this would be it…we've looked everywhere else."

"Do you want to try to break in like we did that one house?" asked Lyra. Tobias closed his eyes, hoping and praying that he would hear the answer—

"No, I'm over this. Let's go…well, it's not home. Let's go back. I'm tired."

The three of them started walking back up the driveway. Tobias gave a quiet sigh of relief. Evidently, the three of them had not yet learned to teleport. This didn't entirely surprise Tobias, as teleportation was difficult and dangerous even in the best of times, but it did intrigue him a little bit. How else were the kids supposed to get up to Jefferson from here?

Tobias pondered the possibilities of how the children could have conceivably left the headquarters of the Arcane Rebellion and arrived in Jefferson for a little while before he grew bored with his thoughts. He dozed on and off, as he was often prone to do as of late. He rarely slept hard, instead dozing in small doses—an hour of sleep here, an hour there. Or so he guessed. Time was something that Tobias didn't really have a way to track at this point. Hunter had taken away all the clocks, calendars, anything that could be used to keep track of time. Or at least, Tobias couldn't find anything like that in the house. And he was determined not to ask Hunter anything other than, "When are you going to decide what you're going to do with me?"

He still didn't have a clear answer from the Mexican man. Tobias found himself wondering—almost sympathizing—with Hunter occasionally. Hunter had found himself trapped in a vicious situation. He couldn't just let Tobias go without Sabrina, Lucien, and the other members of the Arcane Rebellion tracking him down. But keeping him here—aside from committing a crime of false imprisonment and/or kidnapping, Tobias wasn't sure which one–couldn't be a fantastic solution either.

Tobias had fallen into a light doze again when Hunter arrived back at the house. Tobias stirred as he heard the door open, and he saw Hunter walk in. It was dark outside; the stars outside seemed to shine bright. It seemed to be the dead of night.

"Good evening, Toby. Did I wake you?"

"Yes," said Tobias. He sat up from his position on the couch. "Have you decided–?"

"No," said Hunter simply.

"Well, you should probably know about those kids coming here and almost seeing me."

Hunter frowned. He closed the door to the house and turned back to Tobias. "Kids coming here?"

"Yes. Elena, Lyra, and Darian."

Hunter swore.

"Did they see you?"

"No, I hid."

This seemed to surprise Hunter. "Why?"

"What do you mean, why?"

"You didn't want them to see you?"

74

"No, Hunter. I didn't want them telling Sabrina or Lucien about me being in your house. I thought that might be kind of hard to explain to your leaders."

Hunter looked at Tobias. "I didn't realize you cared," he said slowly.

"I do, Hunter," said Tobias, rolling his eyes. "But I don't want to be here anymore either."

Hunter understood; despite everything that had happened, Tobias still seemed to care about him. Hunter rather doubted he deserved this level of love from Tobias, but who was he to complain or argue about it?

"Thanks, Toby."

"You can thank me by letting me go."

Hunter smiled at him sadly. "You know I can't, Toby."

"Right."

The two men sat in silence for quite a while at this. Toby started to doze off again when Hunter spoke:

"You don't have to forgive me, you know."

Tobias recoiled, being awoken from his light snooze. "What?" he asked groggily.

"You can be mad at me."

Tobias was startled to hear the tone of Hunter's voice; he

75

was pleading with him.

"What do you mean?"

"Be mad at me, Toby."

"Why?"

"Because...because you should be mad at me!"

Tobias stared at Hunter, confused. "You...want me to be mad at you?"

"Yes!"

"But, why?"

"Because I deserve it."

Hunter put his head in his hands, as though trying to shield his face from Tobias. Tobias sighed.

"Hunter, spit it out. What's wrong?"

"I don't deserve you, Toby."

"I know."

"Well, I don't. I kidnapped you; I've kept you prisoner all this time. I drained you of your magic. I'm...I'm a terrible friend."

Tobias secretly agreed with Hunter. Though he kept his mouth shut.

"I'm going to bed," said Hunter suddenly. "Maybe…maybe I'll have a clearer head in the morning. I have to go meet with the children in the morning."

And he stood up and went to bed. Tobias stared after him, not paying much attention. Then he dozed off again.

Chapter Eight: Where We Are

Hunter awoke. It was really very early in the morning for him to be awake already. He was generally not a morning person, preferring the darkness of the night to ease his pain, as he said. As it was, he rose out of bed and dressed quietly. He was to be teaching Lyra, Elena, and Darian today, and he wanted to be sure of their magical prowess, which would of course mean he needed to be in tip-top shape. Never much for running, Hunter nevertheless left the warmth and safety of his cottage to go for a brisk walk. It was still rather dark outside, he noticed as he looked through the window.

He exited the bedroom and walked down the stairs as quietly as he could. He didn't really want to wake Tobias. The last thing he needed was for the man to question him, again, about what he had decided. However, Tobias was seemingly asleep; after peeking his head into the living room, he saw the man slumped up against the wall, dozing quietly. Hunter smiled at the sight. He loved watching Tobias sleep. He could do it all day. Alas, he had places to be.

Silently, he slipped out of the front entryway and into the yard, closing the door behind him. He began walking up the driveway, maintaining his silence but also walking quickly. Hunter was lost in thought, thinking about everything he and Tobias had been through. Would their friendship survive this?

"You can have the best intentions in the world, and still do harm." Tobias's words, from just a couple of weeks ago, rang in Hunter's ears as if Tobias were saying them into a microphone at a crowded concert. Hunter thought he was starting to see what Tobias had meant by that statement; their relationship–if you could call it that–had never been as strained as it was now. And it was entirely Hunter's fault.

The problem was, Hunter was stubborn. He would be the first to admit this, of course, but he was not one to admit when he was wrong about something. He still felt like Tobias had abandoned him–had chosen the Bellwater Mages, and Aurora of all people–over him. And that was something that just did not sit well with him.

Hunter was walking down the road now. He did this often enough that he was familiar with the landscape, but not so often that it wasn't a little bit unsettling for him to be doing this in the dark. He generally did this more in the afternoon or early evening as opposed to early in the morning. The sun hadn't even risen yet, and he kept feeling like something was tailing him, or keeping tabs on him. Hunter would look over his shoulder, expecting to see someone there, but things were as pitch black as ever, and Hunter would turn around again to continue his walk. However, the feeling kept distracting him. After about twenty minutes of this walk, he decided to just teleport to the Rebellion headquarters. He would get there a little bit early, but there was nothing wrong with that.

He walked in the door to the warehouse and was expecting to see it empty early in the morning. He did not expect to see Sabrina and Lucien in the middle of the entrance, making out. They broke apart as soon as they saw him, but they both smiled at him.

"Hunter! You're here early. We weren't expecting you for quite some time yet."

Sabrina's greeting, though not unexpected, seemed to ring in Hunter's ears for an abnormally long time. He grimaced quickly but turned it into a smile before either of the couple noticed.

"Good morning to the two of you, as well. I wasn't, er, interrupting anything, was I?"

"Yes, as a matter of fact, you were," Lucien replied gruffly, but Sabrina shook him off.

"Oh, don't mind him, Hunter. He's just annoyed because I woke him up earlier than he wanted."

"What are you two doing here, anyway? Don't you have to be at Bellwater?"

"It is the holiday break for students and staff, so we are out of school for a while," said Sabrina sweetly.

"What's the situation like over there, anyway? Are they still looking for Tobias?"

Lucien huffed. "Yes," he grunted. "Aurora and Odion seem determined to find him. They even tried hunting down Ted."

"They did what now?"

"They went to Ted's old neighborhood, where he used to live before joining us, trying to find him. They didn't, of course, but young Marina ran into them—"

"Marina…the blue-haired girl who controls water?"

"The very same. They confronted her two on one and they won, of course. We need to figure out how we are going to get her back."

"What do you mean, get her back?"

"He means they kidnapped her and are holding her hostage," Sabrina answered, no longer sweet but cold as ice.

"But…don't you lead them now, Sabrina? Couldn't you just order them to let her go?"

"She does lead them," Lucien replied. "But Aurora is acting on her own, with a young man named Odion. It appears the others aren't aware that she is up to anything out of the ordinary."

"Do they know about you two?"

"Aurora has suspicions, but she has been unable to prove them," Sabrina said. "I'm letting her keep running her mouth; the others are starting to think she's crazy. I agree with them, of course, but I'm letting her dig her own grave, so to speak. Let them see her for who she is and let her do all the hard work for us."

"That's what we were celebrating," said Lucien. "When you interrupted us, I mean. It seems they've finally hit a breaking point. Aurora has been called in front of the school board to answer for some of the decision-making she's made as principal."

Hunter smiled, a wide toothy grin that he was sure made him appear crazy. "So, she's finally going to answer for the things she's done?"

"Perhaps, Hunter. Perhaps."

Sabrina winked at him, then grabbed Lucien's hand. "I think the two of us are going to head back home, Hunter. You can handle the students today on your own, right?" And without waiting for a reply, the duo vanished into thin air.

"Oh yeah, sure, that's fine," Hunter answered sarcastically into the empty space surrounding him. He sighed and walked to the back of the warehouse, where the training room was held. He did not need to wait long for Elena, Lyra, and Darian to show up. He was surprised to see them this early in the morning, as though they had been up for hours.

"Well, good morning," he said politely. "I didn't expect you three for at least another hour."

"Are we working with you today?" Darian sounded excited. Hunter supposed he didn't blame the boy; from what he had seen of his magical ability, it was there, though needed some oomph to make it go.

"Yes, you're stuck with me today."

Darian cheered. Lyra smiled. Elena snorted.

"He's not all that special," Elena shot back at Darian, looking annoyed. "Don't forget, he's the one who put us here in the first place."

"You're welcome," Hunter replied scathingly.

"That wasn't a—"

"Shall we get started? Now, I'm familiar with what your sister," he nodded towards Elena, "is capable of, but show me, Lyra. What are you capable of?"

The three children were blasted away from each other in about a second. Elena, who had expected nothing less at this point from her instructor, simply used her own magic to stabilize herself and landed gracefully on the other side of the room. Darian went flying towards the back of the room and slammed hard into a concrete wall, a cracking sound coming from his back. Lyra landed headfirst onto the floor where they had been standing, smashing her skull in the process, her hair covered in blood.

"Oh my god!" Elena screamed. Hunter frowned; perhaps he had expected too much too soon. He walked over to Lyra and put his hand over her head. Instantly, all the blood rushed back into her skull and her skull seemed to mend itself. She was dazed and looked terrified at the Mexican man. Elena ran over to Darian, who was screaming in pain.

"It's okay, it's okay, Darian…" she repeated to him in an undertone, as though this would magically make it all better.

Hunter looked Lyra over very carefully before moving on from her. He hadn't expected her to land headfirst onto the floor; it seemed she had tried to stop him and succeeded partially. She had prevented him from blowing her backwards, but the force of his spell was such that she was still pummeled to the ground.

"Good work," he said to her, genuinely. She looked at him, obviously a little dazed. "You would have prevented that altogether with more practice. Take a minute to rest, and we'll try again."

Hunter got up and walked over to Elena and Darian, who was still on the ground with his back thrown out. Hunter looked the pair up and down, and then said calmly, "Heal him, Elena."

"What?"

"Heal him. Mend it. You can do it."

"But I've never–"

"You need to know how to mend wounds. That is the simple fact. We are doing dangerous work here, and you should expect to be attacked at any moment."

"But how do you mend wounds?"

"You perform magic by feeling. Your emotions are what give you your magic. So, to mend wounds, you show emotion towards other people. For example," Hunter leaned down and wrapped Darian into a hug. His sobs subsided almost at once; his shock at being hugged by the man who had just attacked him seemed to be in control now.

"Wait, this is what–that's what Mr. Thornfield did to bring him back to life!"

"Yes," said Hunter calmly, not letting go of Darian.

"You just hug them?"

Hunter scoffed. "It's not just a hug, Elena. Hugs are one way of showing affection, probably the simplest. You make them feel loved. That's what heals them."

"Is that why Sabrina and Lucien are always being overly affectionate and gross with each other?" Lyra asked. She had walked over to see what was going on.

"Yes, they try to hoard their power by constantly refreshing each other. Don't you notice how you feel better after a hug?" Hunter explained.

"What about other ways? Kissing, and…other stuff?"

"I'm not kissing Darian, if you're asking me to."

"No, but would that heal too?"

"Possibly. It depends on how the other person takes it though. A kiss is a lot more likely to offend than a hug is."

"What about non-huggers?"

"You find out what makes them feel loved," Hunter answered simply. "But sometimes the act of doing is enough. Even if you're not really a hugger, hugs can still make you feel better. Our magic flows from one body to the other through a close connection. It doesn't really matter how that happens, but proximity matters. The closer you are to someone, the more likely the magic is to work."

Hunter let go of Darian, who was now looking perfectly normal. He had tear stains down his cheeks, undoubtedly caused by the pain, but now he looked as good as new. He smiled at Hunter.

"Thanks," he said.

Hunter sneered. "Don't thank me. Defend yourself, so I don't have to do that again."

A ball of fire came soaring down from the ceiling and landed very close to Darian. He shouted in surprise.

"Did you forget you're here for training?" asked Hunter savagely. He jumped up and leaped directly in front of the three children. "All three of you—defend yourselves!"

Hunter shot a second ball of fire directly at the kids. Darian scrambled to his feet, Lyra screamed and started to run in the opposite direction of the fire. But Elena held her ground; she sent a ball of fire of her own directly into Hunter's. The balls of fire collided in midair and burned brightly for a minute or two, but eventually just went out on their own.

"Lyra, no running away!" Hunter barked. He swept his hand in her direction; a gust of wind came up and sent her soaring back towards Elena and Darian. She crashed right into Elena; the twins stumbled backwards and fell over onto the ground.

"Your turn, kiddo!" Hunter sang, shooting a second fireball directly at Darian.

Darian concentrated hard, and as he did so, Hunter and the twins felt the ground shake beneath their feet. Suddenly, a piece of the floor shot into the air and hit the fireball, extinguishing the fire almost instantly. Darian gasped and then collapsed back on to the wall again.

"Not bad, kid," Hunter grunted. He turned back toward the twin girls. He snapped his fingers; thick strands of fire appeared and flew directly at Elena. The girl screamed and struggled as the strands of fire turned into thick ropes, which tied themselves around Elena, binding her tightly.

"Now you, girlie," Hunter mocked. He threw yet another fireball this time at Lyra. Lyra screamed and flinched; however, a small gust of wind came and caused the fireball to swerve off course, instead going for Darian instead of her. Darian yelled in shock, and the piece of the floor that had shot into the air before did so again, putting the fire out once again. Hunter looked disgruntled, though not surprised.

"You diverted the fireball instead of putting it out? Let's try that again. Probably best not to put one of your classmates in danger, don't you think?"

He conjured another fireball and threw it at Lyra. Lyra didn't flinch this time, instead she concentrated hard and moved her hands the same way Hunter did. This time, the wind was much stronger; it put out the fire before it reached her.

"Good work," said Hunter genuinely. "Homework: practice. I want you all here the day after tomorrow, at the same time for additional training."

Leaving the kids, he turned and walked out of the room.

Chapter   Nine:
Darian Makes Progress

The next few weeks saw Lyra, Elena, and Darian all show remarkable improvement with their magical prowess. The three of them were always on high alert whenever Hunter was in the room with them. He was meeting with all three of them about twice a week and then saw them individually once a week on top of that. It was taking up a fair bit of his time, though he found he minded it less than he thought he would. He enjoyed working with the students—it made him feel like a real teacher again. He had not enjoyed the public school system during his days as a teacher. Not enough time for teaching, too much time spent on other things, if you asked him.

Elena was still very distrustful of him. She had cooled it a little bit with her snide remarks and comments, though she would occasionally still mutter a phrase like, "It's because of him we don't have homes to go back to" or "Our parents would still be alive if not for him." Both perfectly true and valid comments, to be fair, though Hunter was not a sympathetic person; he had been simply following orders. The odd thing was, the other two didn't seem to mind.

Lyra had initially been distrustful of him just as Elena was, though he was finding her to be a lot more forthcoming as of late. She explained to Hunter that Elena had been much closer to their parents than she had been, and that she was taking the loss of their friends hard. Lyra was too, of course, though she had come to terms with the fact that she would need Hunter's help—and the help of the Arcane Rebellion in general—to cope with this, as well as to learn magic to prevent this from happening again.

"They're the ones who did it, Lyra," Elena had retorted, rather rudely. Hunter and Lyra ignored her, as was their custom. He was rather surprised at this behavior, though not nearly as much as Darian's behavior had surprised him. To be frank, Darian's attitude towards magic downright fascinated him.

Darian seemed to be taking the loss of their home, as well as the loss of their friends and families, almost…too well. It didn't really seem to faze him anymore; when the twins would talk about everything they lost, Hunter found Darian seemingly daydreaming or going about and practicing his magic on his own, quietly and out of the way. This was very different from the boy Hunter had seen a few weeks back, who had broken his back with one attack. But now, like the other two, Darian could hold his own against Hunter.

Indeed, the three children together could now hold off Hunter, and had even recently started fighting back against him. They very nearly had him beat too—Hunter predicted his next lesson or two would have the children manage to overpower him and take him out.

Sabrina and Lucien were attending about half of the meetings with the students at this point. It was rare to see one without the other, something Hunter had noticed a long time ago, and a fact that was pointed out one day by Darian during his private lesson with Hunter.

"Sabrina and Lucien are rarely seen apart."

Hunter nodded but didn't say anything.

"I mean, I suppose we saw them as separate people at Bellwater Academy," Darian went on. "But it's…kinda weird. I don't think I've seen one without the other here, ever?"

"Nor have I," Hunter said simply.

"Why is that?"

Hunter pondered this question for a moment. He wasn't sure how much he really wanted to tell him. On the one hand, he was one of his students, and did not rank very highly in the Rebellion. On the other hand, he was a member of the Rebellion, like it or not, and to leave him in the dark about Sabrina's and Lucien's intentions was perhaps not the play either.

"Do you remember, a few weeks ago, when I showed you how to heal wounds?"

"Yes," Darian said quickly. "You told me that…that making people feel loved was the greatest magic of all, or something."

"That's right," Hunter replied. "It is the greatest magic of all. When we make someone feel loved, we pass a magic onto them that is extremely powerful. Fire, water, the elements, they all falter at the power of love. It's cliche," Darian had been smirking at this, "But tell me this. Your back healed very quickly, didn't it?"

Darian nodded slowly. "Yes, I suppose it did. But why don't we just replace all doctors and nurses with hugs then?"

"It's not that simple," Hunter explained. "Not everyone

can do magic, remember. It takes a special kind of person. Someone with above average intelligence, massive amounts of willpower, and something worth fighting for."

"Something worth fighting for?"

"Yes. Surely you fight for something, Darian?"

Darian was quiet for a minute. It appeared he was contemplating his response to Hunter. Then he said, "I suppose I do. I fight to learn magic, to defend myself."

"Oh? What are you defending yourself from?"

Darian appeared sheepish. "Well, I guess I'm not sure," he answered. "Elena keeps going on and on about how you're really the bad guys, but...well, the Bellwater people tried to kill us. So we can't trust them either. I don't think she trusts anyone right now."

"Should she?" asked Hunter genuinely. Darian frowned.

"No, I suppose not."

"I can see where she's coming from. But we're not talking about Elena, Darian. I asked about you."

Darian pondered his response, then said quietly, "Well, I...I kind of like being here, with the Rebellion, actually. Everyone is much nicer here than they were at Bellwater. I know you guys did some bad stuff, and I should be mad at you. But I can't help but trust you?"

Whatever Hunter had been expecting, it wasn't that. He

stared at Darian, dumbfounded.

"I know Mr. Thornfield saved me, brought me back to life and all that," Darian went on. "But I…I don't know. I trust you more for some reason. I feel like you're more honest about your intentions with us. You want us to train in combat to take over Bellwater. I don't really know what Bellwater wants."

Hunter continued to stare at Darian. The boy knew, or suspected, far more than he had expected. The man sighed.

"You're right, Darian," he relented. "The Rebellion's goal is to take over Bellwater. We believe only certain people should have access to magic. Bellwater was designed for anyone to learn magic."

"I knew it!" Darian shouted in reply. "I heard Sabrina and Lucien talk about it a few days ago, but they stopped talking once they saw me," he explained.

"Yes, well, I don't see any point in keeping it from you any longer. The Rebellion wants to stomp out widespread magic use. Only we should have access to magic. It is a great power, and in the wrong hands can do a lot more harm than good." Hunter thought of Tobias when he said this, and his stomach lurched; the man had been ignoring him for the better part of the last few weeks, not saying or eating much. He had hoped that Tobias would have been more receptive to him by now.

"Will Bellwater just teach anyone?"

"No, not exactly I suppose. You still need to show some degree of skill or aptitude with magic. But, well, you saw their 'leader'. And they won't get rid of her. We've tried so many times.

Sabrina, Lucien, even myself. But they fail to see how she's not good for us."

"Then why do they keep her on?"

Hunter thought for a moment. How much was too much to let on?

"Aurora saved Tobias Thornfield's life. Tobias Thornfield is the strongest mage alive."

Hunter realized his mistake as soon as he said it, but hoped against hope that Darian wouldn't catch on. "I should say, he was," Hunter corrected himself, smiling convincingly. Or so he hoped.

Darian looked at him suspiciously. "What did she do?"

"That, I'm going to keep to myself for the time being."

"Mr. Thornfield must have been very important."

"Oh, he was."

"To you?"

Hunter hesitated. "Yes," he said truthfully.

Darian nodded. "That had to be hard. To kill someone you loved."

This was the very last conversation on earth Hunter wanted to have, least of all with Darian, who he didn't really know all that well, all things considered. "An interesting conversation to have with your teacher," Hunter replied casually. "Shall we move on to today's lesson?"

Darian continued to make great strides in his work as usual, but Hunter found himself very distracted during the lesson. After they concluded, Darian thanked him as he always did (Darian was very polite, almost annoyingly so) and they left the room together. Hunter teleported back to his cottage in Jefferson and walked in to find Tobias lying in his usual position in the living room. Tobias looked up as Hunter entered the room.

"Good evening, Toby," Hunter greeted. He looked Tobias up and down. His heart seemed to sink. He hadn't properly looked at the man in weeks it seemed. Tobias, always a little skinny, had shrunk to even smaller proportions. He looked like he hadn't eaten in weeks; he could see the ribs poking out of Tobias's midsection.

"Want something to eat, Toby?"

Hunter went into the kitchen and started making two sandwiches. "I know peanut butter and jelly is your favorite, but I think you need something a bit more substantial. How about turkey and cheese? You liked that too."

Hunter finished putting the ingredients on to the bread and plated the sandwiches. Then he brought them out to the living room. Tobias still hadn't said a word to him.

"Tobias, I am not monologuing here. This is supposed to be a conversation. You know, the thing that takes place between two people where they talk to each other?"

Hunter handed one of the plates with the sandwich to

Tobias. Tobias took it, begrudgingly. Then he took a small bite.

Hunter went and sat down on the couch, facing Tobias. "It's time we talked," he said firmly. "I've made a decision, Toby."

Tobias raised his head in Hunter's direction.

"I've decided...I need to come clean about this. I can't just keep you here. I'm going to let you go."

Chapter Ten: Realizations & Actions

Tobias was stunned.

"You're...you're going to let me go?"

It was very much in-character for Hunter to take a long time to decide. Hunter often came across as cold and calculating, but Tobias knew from experience that this was Hunter's way of protecting himself. What he didn't expect was for Hunter to come to this decision. He fully expected Hunter to kill him. To hear Hunter's plan to let him go was very out of left field for the Mexican man.

"Do you have an objection?"

"No, of course not, Hunter. I'm just...surprised, is all."

Tobias stood up and began pacing the living room. "So, what is your plan?"

"What do you mean?"

"Well, you can't just let me go, Hunter. The Rebellion thinks I'm dead, remember? And besides, I can't do magic right now."

Hunter put his head into his hands. Evidently, this was becoming more complicated than the man had expected.

However, Hunter quickly lifted his head back up and said, "You can have the best of intentions, and still do harm."

"What?"

"That's what you told me, Toby. It's a…it's a lesson I had to learn the hard way, I suppose. But you're right. Kidnapping you, holding you hostage like this…it was wrong of me to do it this way. I was trying to protect you, to save you. But I went about it all wrong."

"I still don't understand what exactly it is you think you're saving me from."

Hunter stood up, went to the kitchen, and returned moments later with a large bowl of water. He set the bowl down onto the floor and waved his hand at it. Instantly, a tall, beautiful woman appeared in the basin: Aurora Wildwood. She was not alone. Tobias saw Odion Montgomery in the background, seemingly trying to distance himself from the happenings. And a blue-haired girl that Tobias didn't know was on her knees in front of Aurora. Aurora was holding a whip-like vine in one hand and seemed to be controlling thorny rose petals with the other. The blue-haired girl, evidently, was being tortured. The two men stared at the apparition, in shock.

"The blue-haired girl is named Marina," Hunter explained slowly. "She's a member of the Rebellion. Evidently, she was captured by your colleagues and is under duress for information. Information on you."

Tobias stared at the image as Aurora whipped her vine at Marina's bare back. You couldn't generally hear scrying images, but Tobias thought he could feel the whip-like sensation on his back as Aurora laid down her whip on to the bare flesh. He flinched, then turned his back on it.

"You can make this up, Hunter. I'm not stupid."

"I'm not lying!"

Hunter was rather defensive about this, which made Tobias stop. Hunter had told his fair share of lies over the years, but if Hunter was lying, he would certainly be a lot less defensive and a lot more level-headed. No, this was the truth. Tobias could read it on Hunter like a book.

Hunter took a deep breath. "I knew…Sabrina and Lucien told me a while back about Marina being kidnapped. They told me they were taking care of it. But it doesn't seem like they are. I had no idea it was this bad." Hunter seemed panicky now as he continued to watch the scene with Aurora and Marina unfold.

"What are you going to do about it?"

"I already told you, Toby. I'm letting you go."

Tobias raised his eyebrows. "What's the catch?"

"What do you mean?"

"I mean, what do you want from me in exchange for my freedom?"

"Nothing," Hunter retorted. "I…I'm sorry."

He stooped down and took a key out from a small pocket. He unlocked the chains binding Tobias to the house. Tobias felt warm; he could feel his magic flowing back into himself. He gave a huge sigh of relief and welcome at the sensation.

Hunter turned away from Tobias. If Tobias didn't know better, he'd swear he saw Hunter shed a tear. Tobias frowned.

"Hunter."

"You should go."

The dismissal was abrupt, but apparent. Tobias stood, shocked at the sudden change in Hunter's attitude. Hunter was known for being rather quick to change his mind on things, but this still surprised Tobias. More than anything, Tobias wasn't sure what to do from here; he couldn't exactly leave the house. It was cold outside; he didn't have reliable transportation to get anywhere. Magic and teleportation would take energy that he simply didn't have yet. It would take time for him to build his strength up again.

"Where am I supposed to go, Hunter?"

Hunter sighed, continuing to face away from Tobias. "You need to stop Aurora, Toby. You're the only one who can."

"So…you're letting me go…to save Marina?"

Hunter turned to face Tobias, for the first time in a little while. He could see, plainly now, that Hunter was on the verge of tears. "No, Toby. I came to this decision a while ago. You need to get out of here. Marina's situation…does complicate things a bit, I will admit. But you still need to get out of here."

"What about Sabrina and Lucien?"

"What about them?"

"They're gonna kill you, Hunter. That's what."

Hunter shook his head. "I don't think so," he said stiffly.

"What makes you so sure?"

"I'm not 'sure' of it, by any stretch of the imagination. But...I have a feeling you're going to see Sabrina and Lucien aren't the enemies here."

Tobias and Hunter continued to stare at each other. Tobias began to grow uncomfortable with how Hunter was looking at him. Tobias had to take several moments to realize what it was; Hunter was looking at him like a man who was deeply in love with him. It appeared Hunter's letting Tobias go was the ultimate sacrifice, like letting a winning lottery ticket go to the next person in line. Tobias supposed he felt grateful for that.

"What are you going to do?"

"I think I'm going to lay low for a while," said Hunter quietly. "I don't think Sabrina and Lucien will kill me, but I don't think they'll be particularly happy either. Best to stay out of the way for a while, I think."

Tobias nodded. "And I'm...I guess I'm going back to Aurora." For the first time in his life, Tobias didn't seem excited about that. Hunter looked at him curiously.

"Isn't this what you want?"

Tobias hesitated. The truth was, seeing Aurora like that was not an easy thing to forget. To delay answering, Tobias asked a question of his own.

"What day is it?"

Hunter glared at him. "It's Christmas Eve." Hunter had long since learned the quickest and easiest way to get Tobias talking was to answer his questions quickly, with no argument. Tobias loved to argue, and he usually won them. This answer, however, seemed to take Tobias aback. He looked at Hunter, shocked.

"Christmas is your favorite holiday. You'd really let me go on your favorite day of the year?"

"I was hoping that once I told you, you'd feel sorry for me and stay for another few days. But then I saw what Aurora was doing to Marina. She's losing it, Toby. You're gonna need to go back and calm her down. Again, isn't that what you want?"

"No," Tobias answered truthfully. He was silent for a moment, then he said quietly, "I'd like my best friend back though."

There was yet another moment of tension between the two men, everything Hunter had done to Tobias seemed to crash into the pair of them like a tsunami.

"Did I just get friendzoned?" asked Hunter. At this, Tobias laughed, and Hunter smiled too. Not his usual smirk, but an actual, genuine smile. Tobias loved to see it.

"Yes," Tobias answered playfully. "Best friendzoned

though, if that makes you feel better."

Chapter Eleven: The Dream

Hunter slept soundly that evening. He was delighted to be on friendly, speaking terms with Tobias again. He wasn't foolish enough to believe that Tobias would forgive and forget about the whole kidnapping and false imprisonment thing, but he did think there was a chance they could move forward with their friendship and possibly move into something more.

He was not usually someone who remembered his dreams, but tonight's dream started out strong and vivid. He was a kid again, back in Mexico. His parents weren't around as usual, and he was left to his own devices at just eight years old. At first, they had tried to get a babysitter, usually his cousin Sean. But Sean now had his own little brother to take care of, and Hunter got forgotten about as per usual. So, he sat in his room, home alone, playing quietly on his Game Boy when there was a knock on the door to the apartment. Hunter froze.

Hunter didn't grow up in the safest part of Mexico. Gangs ruled the streets with the police being deep in their pockets. A knock at the door would be enough to unnerve anyone really. Slowly, Hunter got out of his bed and walked down the stairs.

"Hola?" he said sheepishly.

"¡Hola, niño! ¡Es su vecina!" It was Rosa, Hunter's elderly neighbor lady. He recognized her voice. Little Hunter smiled and opened the door. A nice, elderly woman wearing a sombrero and sundress, Rosa was one of Hunter's favorite people in the whole world. He beamed at her.

"Entra, Rosa," he said politely. He had been raised to always speak politely and respectfully to Miss Rosa. She beamed at him and entered the room as he had invited her to do. He closed the door behind her, and together they walked into the living room.

"Dónde están tus padres, Hunter?" Where are your parents? Hunter sighed.

"No se. Con la pandilla, probablemente." I'm not sure. With the gang, probably.

Miss Rosa did not speak English. At this point, Hunter didn't either. He didn't learn the English language until he was a teenager and had immigrated to America. Miss Rosa frowned at him.

"Lo siento, chico." I'm sorry, little one. Hunter smiled at her.

"Esta bien, Miss Rosa! Esta aqui!" It's all good, Miss Rosa. You're here.

"Lo siento, chico," Miss Rosa repeated. Then she repeated it again. And again. And again. Hunter frowned.

The dream shifted. He was now a teenager again. Tobias was sitting next to him, talking quickly.

"Did you know there's magic in the world, Hunt?! We can go be real-life mages! Wouldn't that be awesome?!"

"What's the catch, Toby?" Always the cynical one, he was.

"I met this awesome woman, named Aurora! Miss Wildwood, I should say. She can make earthquakes happen with a snap of her fingers. She can grow plants and attack people with them. It's like...it's like she's..."

"Who would want to attack people with plants? They're just flowers."

"Don't underestimate her. I saw her—" Tobias stopped and frowned at Hunter, then said sheepishly, "She saved me, Hunt. With her powers."

"She did what now?"

"She saved me. These men...they were coming after me. With baseball bats. And she stopped them. She made vines appear out of the ground and strangled them. Then she made sure I was okay and told me to leave. I think...I think she killed them, Hunt. All for me. To protect me."

Hunter was alarmed. "Why would you be happy she killed people, Toby?"

"You don't understand. They were trying to hurt me, Hunt. You don't want that to happen, do you?"

"Of course not—"

"You don't want that to happen, do you?" Tobias repeated, fading in and out as Miss Rosa had done earlier. "You don't want that to happen, do you?"

105

The dream shifted again. Now Hunter was facing Aurora Wildwood. She towered over him, and it was clear to him she was enraged.

"You leave Tobias Thornfield alone, do you understand me, boy?"

"But why?"

"He doesn't need riff raff like you corrupting his mind. No, I've big plans for young Tobias, don't you worry. Leave here. Leave, and never return."

Hunter ran out of the room; he could feel tears streaming down his face. To be forcibly removed from his best friend's life like that...

Sabrina and Lucien came into focus. They comforted him, reassured him.

"It's okay, Hunter," said Lucien softly, like a proud father. "Don't listen to her. She doesn't understand you like we do."

"Join us, Hunter," Sabrina purred comfortingly. "Don't worry about her. We'll protect you. We'll let you grow and become even stronger. Don't worry about them. We'll protect you."

"We'll protect you," Sabrina and Lucien repeated the words together over and over like Miss Rosa and Tobias had done.

Hunter wanted to scream. He was so confused. Why was

he dreaming all of this? Why was he...

Then the dream shifted once again, and he was back with Miss Rosa. However, he was no longer eight years old. He looked himself up and down; it was the present day, all right. He looked at Miss Rosa. She was exactly as he remembered her. She smiled at him.

"Hello, Hunter."

To hear Miss Rosa speak English shocked him more than anything else had thus far. Then he remembered this was a dream.

"Miss Rosa," he said politely. He wished he could offer her a chair. Then two chairs appeared out of nowhere, squashy recliners that you could sit in for hours. He gestured towards the chairs.

She smiled at him and sat. As she did so, she said calmly, "Always so polite, you were, Hunter. Always made an old woman proud."

"Are you dead?"

He didn't mean to ask the question like that. He hesitated, then clarified, "I'm sorry, Miss Rosa. I never kept in touch with you. I moved to the States to get away from...well, to get away from Mama and Papa, and I never reached out to you again. I'm so sorry. I never learned what happened to you."

"Yes, Hunter. I am dead."

Hunter nodded, and tears started to swell up in his eyes. "I'm sorry I never came to visit you, Miss Rosa."

"What do you think you're doing now, chico?"

He blinked and wiped the tears out of his eyes quickly. "I…I suppose I'm visiting you."

"You're keeping your promise to an old friend," she supplied. "You seem to have made a lot of promises to old friends lately, some you've been able to keep and others maybe not so much." She nodded to Hunter's right. He turned and saw a small basin of water. Tobias's face showed up in the basin. Hunter blanched.

"You've been busy," Miss Rosa said simply. Hunter sniffed and nodded.

"Yeah, I suppose I have been."

He turned to look at her fully. She radiated warmth and kindness. He smiled at her. She had been more family to him than his own parents, that's for sure.

"You're not a bad man, Hunter."

To hear her say those words was like music to his ears. He didn't say anything but looked again at Tobias. His heart hurt, there was no other way he knew of to phrase it.

"You were trying to protect him from someone who, you believe, seeks to do him harm."

Hunter turned and looked again at Miss Rosa. "Aurora," he said firmly. Miss Rosa nodded.

"Does she seek to harm him though?"

"My dear boy, I do not know. I've never met the woman myself. But if your instincts are telling you she has ill intentions, I'd be inclined to believe them."

"What if I'm wrong?"

"Then you made a mistake," she said simply. "In an effort to protect someone you love."

Hunter frowned. "Toby says...I can have the best intentions in the world, and still do harm."

"I did not say you haven't done harm," Miss Rosa responded gently. "I said you made a mistake. Your heart was in the right place, Hunter. That means something."

Hunter nodded, then swallowed. "I just...I just don't know if I deserve Tobias."

"Of course you do. He needs you, and you need him. Now more than ever."

"What can I do?"

"Love him. Love him like you always have, like you always will. Not romantic love," she stopped him before he could interrupt. "No, love is much more complicated than that, Hunter. You can love someone without wanting any kind of romance from them. You can, and should, love your friends, your family, your neighbors," she gestured towards herself. "That, in a way, is the most powerful love of all."

Hunter pondered her words for several minutes.

He turned to face her again. She continued to smile at him, kindly, warmly. She truly had been like a grandmother to him.

"Why did you never marry?"

He realized after asking that question that it might have been insensitive. But she continued smiling at him.

"Romantic love was never my thing, Hunter. I just wanted friends I could love and spend the rest of my days with. I got that. I got that with you."

"Until I abandoned you."

"You did not abandon me," Miss Rosa corrected sharply. "The day you left was the day I died, as a matter of fact. I made a mistake, trying to protect someone I loved. The gangs shot and killed me."

Hunter gaped at her.

"There was nothing you could have done," she went on quickly. "I promise you. I made my own choice. I decided to do what was right, and I got punished for it. Life isn't fair, Hunter. But I made my choice, just as you had done. You can't change it. But you can learn from it." She turned to look at Tobias. "He's not wrong about the sentiment. You can have good intentions, and still do harm. But don't let that undermine the fact that you still had good intentions, Hunter. Good intentions mean something, even if other people don't always see it that way."

Hunter nodded, then smiled at Miss Rosa. "Te amo, Miss

Rosa." I love you, Miss Rosa.

"Te amo, chico."

Chapter Twelve: Confrontation

"Tell us where he is!" Aurora roared with fury, brandishing her vine like a whip. It struck Marina's bare back with such force that her skin, already bruised and torn from repeated lashings, quivered at its touch.

"I swear, I don't know!" Marina screamed, tears rolling down her face. "I don't know where he is! We were told he's dead! I swear to you; we were told he's dead! Stop it!"

Aurora brandished her vine whip again, this time striking Marina across the face. Aurora was furious, her eyes glaring at Marina like daggers. She held out her open hand, and razor-sharp rose petals blew around Marina, cutting and scraping all over her body. Marina looked like she had several hundred paper cuts.

"Aurora," Odion began, but was quickly cut off.

"Shut up, Odion! Don't you care about finding Tobias?!"

"I do, but is this…"

"Yes, this is necessary! We need to find him, and this bitch knows where he is!"

Aurora struck again, this time hitting Marina's leg. There was a sharp crack, and a squeal of pain as Marina hit the floor, cowering and holding her now broken leg. Aurora laughed.

"Tell us where Tobias is, and we may spare your life."

"I don't know."

Tears were streaming down Marina's face. She looked defeated, as though she were ready to give up. Odion hesitated. Aurora scared him, but he needed to do something, or this poor woman was going to die from the torture Aurora was giving her.

"Aurora...please stop."

Aurora turned to face Odion, obvious annoyance spread across her face.

"Will you shut up?"

Odion blinked at her in surprise. "I beg your pardon?"

"You may not care about finding Tobias, but I do, Odion! You're free to go if you don't care about that, but I don't need you telling me how to run this interrogation!"

Odion stood, shocked at Aurora's words.

"So, are you staying or are you going?"

"I don't think she knows anything." Odion sounded terrified, but firm in his opinion.

"She's lying to us!" Aurora practically shrieked, tears rolling down her own face now. "She has to be...she has to know something..."

"I don't think she does, Aurora," Odion said gently. "We

really should let her go…"

"Oh, so she can run back to the Arcane Rebellion and tell them what transpired here?"

"I won't tell," Marina gasped quickly. "I won't…I promise…"

And she fainted, undoubtedly, thought Odion, from sheer pain.

Odion looked from Aurora to Marina. The former was standing, tall and proud, fury etched in her face. Odion wasn't fooled. He could tell, underneath all the anger and hatred, there was something else there. Fear, he suspected. Aurora was genuinely terrified for Tobias. He could relate. What if they didn't find him? Although they had only briefly met, Odion liked the guy and felt he could learn a lot from him.

But he couldn't condone this behavior from Aurora. He genuinely believed Marina didn't know anything, and as far as he could tell, the only bad thing she had done was to try and protect herself from he and Aurora, who had after all, showed up in her neighborhood unannounced looking for an accomplice of hers. However, he was powerless to stop Aurora. He had just started learning magic and was nowhere near the level of a mage like herself. He sighed and turned to look at Marina.

Her long, luscious blue hair was ripped and torn, undoubtedly from the long amount of torture the poor girl was going through. It was difficult to tell where her blood started and the stains from previous torture sessions ended. Her skin was peeling and ripped to shreds in multiple places. Odion knew the only thing keeping her alive was his secret visits to see her, to hold her, to hug her after Aurora had left. Under the pretense of cleaning up, as he told Aurora.

He looked away from her. He couldn't help but feel sympathy for the young woman, who looked no older than he himself. In a different life maybe, they could've been together. But there was no way she would ever accept the idea of being his mate after everything he and Aurora had put her through. He turned to face the woman, who was now in tears.

"Aurora."

"Stop, Odion! I don't...I don't know what to do."

She fell to the floor in sobs. Her screams and cries echoed around the room they were in. Aurora and Odion had brought Marina to the basement of Bellwater Academy. Not many people knew of the basement, which had long since been abandoned. Designed as a tunnel from the school to the hospital for emergency services, the walls and ceiling were heavily insulated, so no one could hear her screams. It truly was the ideal place for someone to lay low and avoid detection. Odion hadn't even known about this place, and he was a teacher at the school. Aurora had known only after exploring every nook and cranny of the place, she had said.

Odion crouched down on the floor and sat beside Aurora. He didn't put his arm around her like he had done Marina, all those times. Rather, he sat beside her rather begrudgingly. But he knew he had to. He had to talk some sense into the woman. One of these times, it would work.

"Aurora, there is no point in keeping her here. Let's let her go."

Aurora sniffled, wiping away her tears, then turned to look at Odion. She looked like crap. Her eyes were bloodshot, tear stains streaked down her cheeks. It looked like she hadn't slept in days.

"We've talked about this at least a dozen times, Odion. You know we can't."

"What's the worst that could happen?" asked Odion defiantly. "We're going to kill her if we keep this up! We have come very close to doing so already!"

Aurora sighed. "I wish there was a way to read minds," she said sadly. Mind-reading was in no way possible. A person's mind was supposed to be their one safe place, away from the harsh realities of day-to-day life. Odion, of course, knew this was a fantasy. Expecting someone to not deal with personal demons was like believing in a world with dragons and monsters. No, sadly. The only monsters around here were the people and their thoughts.

"Aurora, I know you think you're doing the right thing," said Odion firmly. "I know you think she knows something. I know you think that by keeping her here, you will get information out of her or force the Rebellion to come looking for her. But neither of those things have happened. It's been several weeks since we brought her here. I think we need a new plan."

Aurora looked conflicted for a moment, as though she was struggling internally. Then she sighed again. "Okay, Odion. I'm open to suggestions. What do you think we should do?"

Odion was stunned. He hadn't expected this to work. He

had been trying for weeks to get her to listen to him, and she had just now decided to? He took a deep breath and said quickly, "Let's let her go. Let's follow her. See where she goes. Surely, she'll lead us to the Rebellion?"

Aurora turned to face Odion, frowning. "Tracking her is easier said than done, Odion. One of us would need to be scrying her pretty much all the time."

"Do you think Agatha or Matilda would help us?"

Aurora shook her head. "They're busy with schoolwork. And besides, I'm not sure I trust them to not go blabbering to Sabrina or Lucien. Neither one of them were—are—particularly close to Tobias."

Odion nodded. "Then we do it ourselves. She's weak, Aurora. Surely the two of us could handle scrying her?"

"Do you really believe letting her go in this condition wouldn't kill her, Odion?"

Odion paused. He honestly hadn't considered that.

"We would need to either heal her, which is insanely risky for us not only to give her her power back right now but also for success in tailing her. Or we would need to take her to the hospital, which will have doctors asking us questions. We were just there not that long ago, after Toby was shot. Remember?"

"Of course I remember, Aurora."

The two sat in silence for several minutes, thinking. Odion thought there surely had to be a way out of this. Protect himself,

Marina, and Aurora.

"We could just kill her," Aurora suggested timidly.

Odion turned to look at her, frowning. "I believe that's what's going to happen if we keep her here, Aurora."

"No, I mean. Stop torturing her and just kill her. Leave her down here. No one will ever find her–"

The doors blasted off their hinges at that moment. Aurora and Odion looked. Three people were at the top of the stairs. Odion gulped: Sabrina Braithwaite, Lucien Rodson, and a large, balding man Odion didn't know. The two of them jumped up.

"Sabrina!" Aurora barked.

A large arrow made entirely of fire flew directly at Aurora. She jumped out of the way just in the nick of time. Aurora swore, then flicked her wrist towards Sabrina. Roses, just like the ones used to torture Marina with sharp edges and thorny vines, flew themselves at Sabrina and surrounded her. They cut her, digging into her skin like ants burrowing under the ground. Sabrina screamed, startled, then conjured up little embers that attacked the roses. They crumbled instantly.

Odion looked away from Aurora and Sabrina and found himself face-to-face with Lucien Rodson. He trembled a little bit at the sight of the man.

"Odion," Lucien said simply. "Don't make this harder on yourself."

Out of the corner of his eye, Odion saw the third,

mysterious man kneel down over Marina. He sighed. At least she would be alright. He held up his hands, recognizing defeat.

"Don't hurt me, Lucien."

"Not my intention, kiddo."

The two of them turned to watch the dueling women. Aurora was furious and had conjured up her vine whip, cracking it at Sabrina. Sabrina dodged it with evident ease, using her fire power to burn the whip in places. It started out long and thorny but quickly started to lose some of its size and sharpness. Rose petals continued to swarm the pair of them, though it was impossible to make out which one was really winning the fight.

By all normal laws of magic, fire should have the advantage against grass and plants. But Odion knew better. Aurora was no pushover; she would not go down so easily.

"WHERE IS TOBY?!" screamed Aurora right at Sabrina. Sabrina smirked as though she were enjoying herself.

"He's dead, on my orders, Aurora! He's dead, and you'll never see him again!"

"NO!"

There was an explosion in the middle of the room, and Odion was sent flying backwards. He hit the wall directly behind him. He saw Lucien and the other two people get blown backwards as well from the explosion. Odion stumbled upwards, dazed, and looked around; he could see nothing but dust and smoke.

Suddenly, he felt the ground beneath him tremble. It seemed to be opening. The entire earth seemed to be filled with Aurora's rage. He felt the building sink into the ground, quickly, as though it were enveloped by quicksand. But he could do nothing to stop it. Nothing to protect himself…

In an act of desperation, Odion flung his hands through the air as though wiping away a troublesome smudge on a glass window, and the smoke and rubble cleared. Sabrina and Aurora were revealed, still fighting each other. Aurora had seemingly conjured a second thorn and was striking Sabrina with it much the same way she did Marina. However, Odion noticed Sabrina was fighting back, unlike the blue-haired girl. Sabrina was dealing just as much damage to Aurora.

Odion tried to teleport away but found he couldn't. Whether that was due to the Anti-Teleportation Spell he and Aurora had put around the place to prevent Marina's escape, or whether it was due to Sabrina and Lucien, he was unsure. He was now helplessly watching as Sabrina and Aurora continued to fight it out. He saw the unknown man scoop Marina up into his arms and carry her up the stairs, to safety presumably. Lucien was on the ground, struggling to get up. Odion made a split-second decision to help him stand up. He ran over to him and extended an arm, trying to be helpful. Lucien took it gratefully and pulled himself to a standing position. The two men nodded at each other, then turned and watched the women continue to fight.

"You won't get the best of me, Aurora!" Sabrina snapped, fire crackling at her fingertips as rose petals danced around her, Aurora's vine cracking inches away from her body. Aurora laughed, a cold, merciless laugh that ran shivers down Odion's spine.

"I already have, Sabrina!"

And in that moment, Odion knew that Aurora was about to land a devastating blow. He was not disappointed; Aurora's whip had finally found its mark. It penetrated Sabrina's fiery shield and smacked her, hard, across the face. Sabrina screamed in pain and was sent flying backwards, smashing into a wall. Lucien roared.

"You bitch!"

Lucien charged at Aurora, the power of the wind propelling him forward. His tackle attack met its mark; Aurora was sent flying backwards and she herself fell to the ground in a heap. The school trembled at the force of the blow. Odion stared at her, sure she must be dead. She was bleeding from her head. Even Aurora didn't deserve to be taken out like this…

Sabrina was limping towards Lucien, massaging her cheek where the vine had struck. She smiled weakly at the man.

"Thank you, Lucien. Though I think you overdid it a bit."

She turned and faced Odion. "Hello, Mr. Montgomery," she said sweetly. "You're going to come along with us."

Chapter   Thirteen:
The Teenagers Revolt

"Hunter! Hunter! Wake up!"

Hunter stirred, then his eyes flickered open. Tobias was watching over him, a look of panic in his eyes. Hunter blinked several times; he felt tears in his eyes.

"Hunter, wake up. Someone's here!"

"What?"

"I said someone's here, Hunter! They're outside!"

Hunter jumped out of bed, nearly knocking Tobias aside as he did so. Quickly and quietly, he moved downstairs to the living room. He peered around a corner and indeed heard it as well; three distinct, very familiar voices standing right outside the door to the house.

"He was hiding something! This might be worth checking out after all. Come on, Elena. Lyra."

Hunter swore under his breath. It was Darian and the twin girls. They had come back, to discover his secret it sounded like. He didn't have time to do much more than that before the door came crashing down. Hunter frowned. They weren't very sneaky, were they?

The girls stumbled into the cottage first, looking around cautiously. Darian followed them, an excited grin on his face. It seemed he was the ringleader here, with the girls following alongside him for some reason. Hunter ducked behind his corner again and smirked. They may not be very stealthy, but he sure could be. When he wanted to be. Which, admittedly, was seldom, though not never.

"What are your secrets, teacher?" he heard Elena whisper into the darkness. Then he heard her take a sharp breath. "You guys, come check this out!"

He heard Lyra and Darian tiptoe over to the other twin, though again for tiptoeing, thought they could learn a thing or two.

"Chains," he heard Lyra breathe.

"What for?" asked Darian.

"More like, who for," Elena corrected. "Someone's been here."

"How can you tell?"

"There's crumbs and stuff all over the floor here. He…he's had someone chained up here! For a while too, it looks like."

Hunter heard Darian whistle. Inwardly, he rolled his eyes.

Then, a crash came from upstairs. The teenagers looked up toward the ceiling, their expressions hard to make out in the darkness.

"Was that him, do you think?"

"Or his prisoner?"

"Only one way to find out," Darian declared bravely. Then the boy took a step toward the stairs, where Hunter lurked.

Hunter didn't give the teens time to react. He snapped his fingers, and fire erupted all around the cottage. The girls screamed in shock. Darian yelled. Elena managed to jump out of the way, pulling her boyfriend with her, but Lyra was not so lucky; she groaned in pain as the flames engulfed her entire body.

"What do you think you're doing, children?" Hunter asked, loud enough to be heard but keeping to the dark corner. He had a rather bad feeling about this. He flicked his wrist, and an apparition of himself appeared out of nowhere on the other end of the house. The apparition walked towards the kids, distracting them long enough for him to peer around the corner. The exact same strategy he used with Tobias all those months ago…

"We're going to learn your secret, Hunter," Elena snapped back. "You're hiding something from us, and we want to know what it is!"

She threw a ball of fire directly at the apparition. The real Hunter flicked his wrist again, and the apparition held up a hand, absorbing the fireball with ease.

"What makes you so sure I have a secret?"

"Explain the chains, then!" Elena growled.

"Would you like to find out what they're for?"

The apparition snapped its fingers, and the chains sprang to life. They extended and wrapped themselves around Lyra, who screamed in pain from the hard cold metal wrapping around her burnt skin. The chains clicked into place, and Lyra was secured. Hunter snapped his fingers again, and the chains began to drain Lyra of her magic just as they had done Tobias. Lyra shivered suddenly. This started the two remaining teens, and Darian took a running leap towards the chains, using the power of the wind to propel him forward.

Hunter had seen Lucien fight enough times to recognize his style of attack and thought perhaps that Sabrina and Lucien had arranged for Lyra and Darian to hold back some of what they had been taught during their demonstrations. He sighed and snapped his fingers. Additional chains appeared out of the ceiling and caught Darian as he rushed towards Lyra, capturing him and binding him in place. Another snap of Hunter's fingers, and Darian too began to have the magic drained out of him.

The apparition began to walk towards Elena, slowly but confidently. Elena seemed to grimace, walking backwards, nearly falling over a toppled chair but steadied herself. Ready for a fight.

"You can't win, Elena," the apparition mouthed, the real Hunter saying the words aloud.

Elena looked around the burning room. Hunter had put out most of the fire, and virtually all the damage had been cosmetic. But it still seemed to trigger something in her. She looked around, fearful. Then Hunter recognized it for what it was: post-traumatic stress disorder. She looked on the verge of a panic attack.

"Elena," Hunter said gently. "It's alright. I'm going to let the three of you go—"

"Go where?" Elena laughed, then started to cry. "Go where? Back to being your prisoners?"

"You are not my prison—"

"Like hell we're not! You kill our families and friends, then you kidnap us from the person who saved us! And you expect us to believe we're not your prisoners? Are we free to go?"

Hunter hesitated, then he saw a movement out of the corner of his eyes; Tobias had appeared at the top of the stairs, listening in. He glared up at the man, not entirely sure Tobias could see him, but sure he could feel his gaze.

"I am—we are—trying to help you, Elena! We see potential in you, potential that no one has seen before—"

"My basketball coach saw potential in me! She thought I could maybe go pro!"

"I mean potential with magic, Elena. There's so much untold potential with you—"

"I don't want it!" She practically stomped her foot in frustration. "I don't want magic! I want to go back to being a normal kid, playing basketball with her friends! Worrying about college applications, scholarships, and Homecoming games! I want to go back to being most worried about who's going to ask me out to the prom! I want to be normal!" She shrieked the last word as though hoping it would be an insult. Hunter paused, not sure what to say.

"Elena."

Tobias had spoken, and Hunter swore under his breath. Why did Toby have to speak up? Elena stopped her tantrum, looking bewildered. Even Lyra and Darian–who had been struggling against the chains–stopped momentarily at hearing Tobias' voice.

"Mr. Thornfield? Is that you?"

"Tobias," Hunter growled menacingly. Tobias ignored him.

"Children, listen to me very carefully. I'm sorry. I'm so sorry. For everything. I wish...I wish I could take it all back. But I can't. This is my fault. I was the one priming you up for magic, and I'm the one who told the Bellwater Mages you might have potential. Hunter must have found out about it somehow. We have a mole in our ranks. But I never wanted this. I need you to understand that. I never wanted you to go through all of this, all of this hardship. I never wanted to see your families get killed, your friends get tortured. I never wanted to see anyone get hurt. All I ever wanted was...to see all of you succeed. I did everything I could to make that happen. You're right, Elena. Magic is a tool. Nothing more, nothing less. If you don't want to use it, no one is saying you need to. You just...I need you to understand I'm sorry."

"I'm the one Hunter's been keeping prisoner. He told your team that I died, that he killed me. He lied to you. He's been trying to keep it a secret, but he couldn't bring himself to kill me. There's good in him. There's so much good in Hunter that he would never admit. But he's not a bad person, despite what you may have been led to believe. He's...he's good."

"So, please, children. Please. Find it in your hearts to forgive me. I know I don't deserve it. I know I indirectly caused all your pain and suffering. I know I deserve to die, and I know the world would be a better place if I just...ended it myself. But perhaps more importantly, please forgive Hunter. He did all of this to try to protect me, and to try to protect you from someone else who may not have your best intentions at heart. He...his intentions were pure. He went about it entirely wrong, and he went well over the line with his actions. But he meant to do good. Please, forgive him. Hunter loves, he loves so deeply and so much. Have you ever loved someone so much that you end up hurting them, inadvertently? I have. And Hunter has too. That's what this is, a testament to how much Hunter loves the people he surrounds himself with. He loves you, Elena, Lyra, Darian. He really does. And he loves me too. Even if he has a weird way of showing it."

Tobias' monologue was met with complete and utter silence for several minutes.

"Let us see you, Tobias," Elena called out. "Show yourself! Prove to us you're not a hallucination brought on by Hunter."

Hunter let out a deep sigh, and nodded towards Tobias, who was already walking into the open living room, hands held up in a sign of surrender. He heard the children gasp when they saw him. Tobias knew he looked like crap, not having bathed, eaten, or slept in days.

Hunter spared a glance at the children. Lyra looked dumbfounded, Elena furious. It was Darian who surprised him, however. He didn't show any sign of surprise or intrigue. If anything, he looked rather bored.

"Yeah, I figured he was holding you here, Mr. Thornfield," Darian said scathingly. Hunter blinked a few times. He was surprised how cold Darian was acting towards his former teacher. Evidently, Tobias was also startled. He seemed to stop in his tracks and turned to look at Darian. The young man was holding back tears with extreme difficulty.

"Darian, what–"

"Why couldn't you just let me die?!"

The words were shouted, and almost echoed throughout the room with how powerfully Darian had shouted them. Hunter watched in shock as Tobias took a step back from his former student.

"Darian, I–"

"YOU SHOULD HAVE LET ME DIE!" Darian roared. "YOU SHOULD HAVE LET ME DIE! INSTEAD, YOU BROUGHT ME BACK TO LIFE–AND FOR WHAT? SO I CAN 'SERVE' THESE...THINGS?!" He gestured around the small house. "These...these MONSTERS!"

Tobias seemed to be quickly losing what little composure he had left. The man was backing away more quickly now and had bumped into more than one piece of furniture, almost toppling over. Hunter was so busy watching Tobias and Darian, he hadn't spared much of a glance at the twin girls.

The twins had ducked out of sight and had come up to right behind Hunter. They turned to each other, nodded, then in unison, attacked the man. Elena launched a powerful ball of fire at him, while Lyra delivered a bolt of lightning at his backside.

Hunter grunted as he felt the force of the fireball hit him. The fire itself wouldn't hurt him, but the force with which Elena struck him winded him. Lyra's lightning bolt, however, struck him down. He collapsed in a heap on the floor and moved no more.

The twins high-fived each other, then moved towards Tobias. Together with Darian, they cornered their former teacher. They laughed as Tobias snapped his fingers, and nothing happened.

"Now then, Mr. Thornfield," Darian said contemptuously. "You're coming with us."

Chapter Fourteen:
Revenge is Served

Tobias glared at the teenagers.

"You really don't know what you're doing, do you, children?" he asked, almost casually. Though there was a definite coldness to his voice now.

"No, I think we're perfectly aware of what's going on here, thank you!" Elena snapped. "This is perfect though. Better than I could have guessed, even!"

"What makes you say that?"

Elena's face broke into a grin. "I knew Hunter had a secret. I didn't realize it would be...you, Mr. Thornfield." She spat out each syllable of his last name as though they tasted like dirt on her lips. Tobias was rather hurt by this.

"Why are the three of you so upset with me?"

"I already told you!" Darian had calmed down a little bit, but was still very close to shouting, "You should have let us die! Instead, we're being held captive by these rebellion folks!"

Tobias blinked. "You're being held captive? I don't see you in chains. In fact, it seems to me like you are free to do whatever and go wherever you please."

Lyra rolled her eyes. "You don't get it, do you? We can't. Not really. We were forced to go along with you and then forced to go along with him--" she pointed a finger at Hunter's lifeless form, "--so you'll forgive us for not being so thankful."

"I saved your lives!" Tobias exclaimed, exasperated. "Did you actually expect me to just let you all die?"

"You saved us, but you didn't save any of our friends or families!" Elena was practically shrieking. "You should have done more! You could have done something to help them!"

"Like what, exactly?" Tobias snapped back. "It was three on one, if I recall correctly--"

"And you took all three of them out with a snap of your fingers!" Darian roared. "Stop the bullshit, dude. You could have stopped this! You could have stopped ALL OF THIS!" Darian actually kicked Hunter in frustration. Tobias heard a painful-sounding crack in Hunter's ribs.

"That's enough, children!" Tobias roared back. "You will not tell me what I should or should not have done! You don't think I live with that, every minute of every day? You don't think I think about the people that died, at the hands of my best friend? You don't think I--"

"We don't care!" Lyra screamed over the teacher. "We don't give a flying--"

"YOU SHOULD!"

It was now becoming difficult to discern who was talking over whom. All four parties--Tobias, Lyra, Elena, and Darian--

were screaming at the top of their lungs, Tobias at the three of them, the three teenagers at their former teacher. After several minutes, Tobias stopped yelling back; instead, he allowed the teenagers to say their fill, make their insults, and get it out of their systems. He did, however, reflect on the words they were saying to him, and he pondered the words he had adamantly told Hunter the last several weeks.

"You can have the best intentions in the world, and still do harm."

He had said the words aloud unintentionally, and he just so happened to say them during a moment of silence. The teenagers, about to go off on him again, stopped their shouts and yells and stared at Tobias.

"You can have the best intentions in the world, and still do harm." Tobias repeated the mantra yet again, then turned to face the children. "I'm sorry," Tobias said again. "I'm...I'm sorry I saved you. My intention was...to get you away from the danger I perceived. I did not think about the long-term consequences of doing so. I'm sorry."

He then turned to Darian. "And I'm sorry to you as well, Darian. Maybe you're right. Maybe...maybe I should have let you die."

Darian scoffed at his former teacher, then turned to the twins. "Are we believing this?" he asked them. It was clear from his tone that he did not believe it.

Tobias turned to see the twins shake their heads. He sighed.

"Okay. Then what now? Are you taking us to Sabrina and Lucien? The ones holding you hostage?"

"Of course," Elena said simply. "You're our ticket to freedom, Tobias."

Tobias raised his eyebrows. "Is that so? How do you reckon?"

"Sabrina and Lucien went to capture Aurora, Tobias," Lyra retorted. "They'll be back at headquarters by now. We will simply take you there."

"And how will you do that?"

"We have a car," Darian replied simply. At this, Tobias laughed.

"How far away are we from your headquarters, Darian? How many hours will it take you to get us there? You really think you can hold two adult mages—Bellwater and Rebellion trained, as it is—for that long? Even now, my power is growing stronger—" he snapped his fingers, and a small jolt of electricity came down and shocked Darian, making him jump— "and you'll have to pass through many people to get us down there. We can simply have the police come by and help us."

The teenagers stood in frustration over this news. There was silence for several long minutes, then Lyra said quickly, "Let's move out. The sooner we get to Sabrina and Lucien, the better."

And they took off, the three teenagers in charge, their old teacher Tobias in tow. For good measure, they brought along the unconscious Hunter, despite Tobias's warnings. It seemed the teenagers had nothing to lose.

The girls had gotten into the back seat of the car with Tobias sitting between them. Darian had wanted to put him and Hunter in the trunk, but the three of them had decided against putting anyone in the trunk. It is far easier to control the people sitting in the car cab than the trunk. Hunter was left to sit shotgun to Darian. Inwardly, Tobias thought this was a plan waiting for disaster. All it would take would be one stop, one bathroom break, one fuel fill up.

Two hours later, according to the clock on Darian's radio, a fabled stop had never come. Hunter was still out cold. And Tobias was starting to lose hope of ever getting out of this situation. The foursome had spoken very little over the last two hours. Tobias had started out strong in hopes of getting them to see reason, though his hopes were quickly dashed. The girls seemed adamantly opposed to anything resembling mercy on behalf of Tobias. So, after a while, he had simply begun to sit in silence with the rest of the group.

"I could go for something to eat," he offered feebly. Darian laughed.

"Don't think we're falling for that. You just want us to stop so you can try to get away."

This was only partially true; Tobias truly was famished. Although it was also true that Tobias was hoping for an easy escape route. It appeared things wouldn't be so simple.

"I really am starving, Darian. He didn't really feed me for…what month is it?"

"January."

Tobias blanched.

"So, many weeks then."

"Yes."

"Come on. You wouldn't want your favorite teacher to starve, would you?"

Darian shifted in his seat. Out of the corners of his eyes, Tobias saw the twins exchange looks.

"Ya know, Darian, I could also go for a quick bite," Lyra offered.

"NO!"

It was Elena who spoke very suddenly and loudly. It seemed as though the twins weren't as in sync as Tobias had thought.

And so, the drive continued. Tobias found himself wishing for Hunter to wake up, perhaps against his better judgment. He knew he should feel angry with his friend, betrayed at the injustice of losing an entire holiday season. But something about Hunter made it difficult to stay mad at him. He wasn't entirely sure Hunter waking up would be a good thing. He was quite sure that Hunter could take out all three teenagers in a fight single-handedly, though he was unsure he wouldn't go overboard and kill them all. He didn't want that, no.

In another hour, though it seemed much longer to Tobias,

he noticed they were approaching the coast. He recognized the port he and Odion had visited back in the fall. It looked much different now in the winter, during the off-season. It almost looked abandoned. It made Tobias feel suddenly much sadder and lonelier. He did miss Odion too. Where was the man now? Did he ever learn more about magic? Tobias hoped for the best for him, though now he had more pressing concerns. Like what was going to happen to him.

Darian parked the car, and the teenagers exited the vehicle. Elena practically dragged Tobias out of the car. He gasped as she pulled on his ear.

"I'm coming, I'm coming, leave me alone!"

It took all three of Darian, Lyra, and Elena to lift Hunter out of the passenger side door and stand him upright. Darian, not an athlete, couldn't carry him by himself, so instead opted to drag Hunter behind him using a rope they had taken out of the trunk of the car. Tobias grimaced. Hunter seemed no closer to waking up now than he had done before they left the cottage.

"What is this?"

Tobias's heart sank. He turned and found himself face-to-face with Sabrina Braithwaite and Lucien Rodson.

Chapter Fifteen: Two Wrongs...

The pair of mages stared at Tobias. He stared back at them. It seemed like time had stopped for a moment as the three of them looked at each other, shock apparent on Sabrina and Lucien's faces. Tobias was sure he was showing some trepidation, perhaps even outright fear at the sight of them. At full power, taking them on would be more than feasible, but in his current state...

"Miss Braithwaite! Mr. Rodson!"

Lyra, Elena, and Darian appeared. For all intents and purposes, they may as well have teleported out of nowhere. Tobias jumped a little bit, moving instinctively closer to the car and away from all five individuals. He hit the car and nearly fell over in surprise; he had forgotten about it momentarily.

Sabrina and Lucien looked at each other, still dumbfounded. Then Lucien pointed a stubby finger at Darian and said coldly, "Explain."

That he did; Darian told them about how he and the twins had followed Hunter to his house and discovered that Hunter had kept Tobias' survival and imprisonment a secret from them for the last few months. While Darian spoke, Tobias slowly inched away from the five mages as quickly as he dared, though Sabrina kept throwing glances his way.

Unfortunately, Darian finished his explanation rather quickly. Tobias hadn't quite reached around the passenger seat to wake Hunter up. If he could just wrap his arm a little bit more around the seat...

"So, what do you say, Tobias?" Sabrina asked him. "Does Darian's version of events line up with yours?"

Tobias jumped. "Er..." he began. Then, his heart leapt; he felt Hunter begin to move around in the car. He just had to keep Sabrina distracted for a while.

"I wasn't really listening, I suppose, Sabrina," Tobias replied quickly, in the most matter of fact, teacherly voice he could muster. "But it all started after our teachers' union meeting a few weeks back, when you were voted to replace Aurora." Tobias had a sudden realization here. "You...you planned that." It wasn't a question; it was a statement. Sabrina and Lucien smiled at him.

"You just now realized that did you?" the man asked, smiling widely. "Yes, it was intentional. Sabrina was to take over Bellwater leadership and command those mages. Then, Hunter was to dispose of you. It seems half of the plan went off without a hitch, but the other half–"

"Where is Hunter?" asked Sabrina suddenly. She directed her question to Darian, but Elena spoke.

"In the passenger seat of the car."

Lucien and Sabrina glared at Tobias. "Step away from the car!" Lucien barked. They were suddenly frightful. Tobias, however, didn't step away.

"I said get away from the car!" Lucien growled. "I'm not going to ask you again!"

Tobias stood his ground, thinking fast. Sabrina and Lucien had many faults, but he was confident they could–and absolutely would–kill him and Hunter if they felt threatened.

Lucien snapped his fingers, and Tobias wrenched the passenger side car door open as fast as possible. Not a second too soon; a gust of wind almost blew him away, but the wind wasn't strong enough to blow the whole car. Tobias held on for dear life as the car door swung in the wind. His heart leapt again when Hunter sat upright.

"Hunter!" Tobias screamed. He heard Lucien curse under his breath, and Sabrina directed her open palm towards the car.

A dazzling bolt of flames flew from Sabrina's outstretched palm and collided with the car's gas tank. Not a moment too soon, Hunter jumped out of the car, caught Tobias like a superhero, and the two of them landed on the ground, hard.

The car exploded. Tobias heard Darian scream, the twins yelled as they ran away from the explosion. Car parts were flying all over the place, and Hunter just barely managed to put up a fiery shield to avoid the glass from the windshield–shattered, no doubt, by the force of the sudden explosion–from striking himself and Tobias in the face.

Tobias turned and saw Sabrina and Lucien

approaching them. Car debris was blowing away from the two of them effortlessly, as though its sole mission was to avoid them at all costs. The pair were staring down at himself and Hunter. He spared a glance at the Mexican man; he was panting heavily. It seemed that protecting him and Tobias was taking a lot out of him.

Hunter glanced back at Tobias. There was something odd about the way Hunter was looking at him. Tobias had to take a second to register what that look was about, but he recognized it: it was, unmistakably, love. Hunter's love for Tobias is what prompted him to emerge from a car, half-unconscious, and protect him with everything he had. Tobias felt a sudden rush of energy flow through him. And he realized, almost too late, what had happened.

Love is the source of all magic. If someone feels unloved, unwanted, their magic fades into obscurity, and they lose the ability to cast spells. Anyone can perform magic, if they feel loved, wanted, and valued in life. Hunter had taken Tobias away from his life, his friends, and isolated him for weeks and weeks, making Tobias feel alone. Although it was true the magic chains certainly drained him of energy, and allowed personal demons to enter his mindset, this may never have happened if Tobias had felt loved by Hunter. Looking back at the last few weeks, Tobias could not honestly say he felt loved by his former best friend. Until now.

With a sudden rush of energy, Tobias grabbed on to Hunter and embraced him. The two hugged, and Hunter, realizing what was going on, sighed and rested his head on Tobias' shoulder.

"It's okay," Tobias murmured, scratching Hunter's back. "It's okay. I've got this."

With more care than was strictly necessary, Tobias laid Hunter down on the ground. Then he turned to face Sabrina and Lucien. The two of them were smiling at him, looking at their prey as though he had been captured and cornered. That couldn't be further from the truth.

"We'll take it from here, Tobias," Sabrina said playfully. "You don't have to fight anymore, darling. You're free to go!"

This last sentence caught Tobias off guard.

"I'm...what?"

"You're free to go! Unless you have some objection?"

"Leave this place, and never return," Lucien chimed in. "We think you've been through enough."

Something was definitely up with this; Tobias could smell it a mile away.

"Just leave Hunter," Sabrina said sweetly. "And you can go."

"Of course," Tobias said aloud, smiling at the pair of them now. "You want to punish him for not killing me. Is that it?"

Sabrina and Lucien both smiled at Tobias, but didn't say anything.

"Where's Aurora?"

Tobias remembered, quite clearly, Lyra telling him that Sabrina and Lucien had captured his friend. He hadn't forgotten it, though he clearly couldn't do anything about it at that time either. Now, he could. He would. He had to.

The smiles disappeared from Sabrina and Lucien's face quickly, as though Tobias had drawn them on with a pencil and subsequently taken an eraser to them.

"Why do you care?" Lucien was rather rude and abrasive in his response, quite unlike the man who had invited Tobias to his students' art gallery. "She abandoned you, didn't she? Didn't even look for you?"

"I find that incredibly difficult to believe," Tobias said cheerfully. "Aurora is always, annoyingly so, right on top of me, it seems."

Sabrina stretched her palm out again, and just like before, a searing bolt of fire went flying towards Tobias. He laughed as he held out his own palm. The tornado that erupted from his own palm disintegrated Sabrina's bolt of fire as though it were merely a lit candle, and it was Tobias' birthday. The tornado slammed into Sabrina, hard, and she was sent flying backwards. She landed on the parking lot pavement and moved no more. Tobias highly doubted she was dead, though she would surely be unconscious for a few hours.

Lucien roared and charged at Tobias. Using the wind to propel himself forward, Lucien's slam was met with one of Tobias's own. The two men collided, and Lucien also went flying backwards. For good measure, Tobias sent a bolt of lightning after the man as well. It crackled and whipped through the air like a missile that had been ready for war months ago and was just now launched. It struck Lucien right in the back, burning his shirt right off his back. His big belly slammed into the pavement right next to Sabrina, and he too, moved no more.

Tobias turned and saw Darian, Lyra, and Elena hurrying towards him.

"Where's Aurora?" he asked the teenagers. The three of them stared at him; Darian seemed as though he were preparing an attack. Tobias laughed.

"Children, I am ready to fight you. I am ready to kill you if I must. Tell me where my friend is."

The teenagers continued to look at Tobias with extreme caution, though they didn't say anything.

"I'll let you go," Tobias said quietly. "I'll let you go, and you'll never hear from any of us again. I promise. Just tell me where Aurora is."

"She's in the building," Lyra said quickly. "She and Odion are both in there, chained up."

Tobias nodded, then turned towards Hunter. He was breathing heavily; it seemed as though he had fallen asleep. Tobias frowned. "I should probably–"

The Earth shook a little bit. He turned, frowning, as

he saw Darian slam his foot into the ground.

"Darian, what are you–"

Tobias managed to teleport out of the way just in time; a massive tremor split the ground he had been standing on in two. Tobias cursed, then snapped his fingers. A bolt of lightning came down and struck Darian where he stood. He screamed as electricity rippled through his body. Then he collapsed on the ground and lay motionless. The girls screamed. Elena went and shook him.

"He's...he's not breathing!"

Tobias stood in silence as the girls both panicked over Darian's lifeless body. True to form, Tobias killed the boy. It seemed that's what Darian wanted. He didn't want freedom from the Rebellion, or Bellwater, or magic in general. He wanted freedom from life.

"Bring him back!" Elena roared at Tobias. "Bring him back NOW!"

Tobias blinked, then said sadly, "He wouldn't want that, Elena. Remember?"

Elena pulled her hair in frustration; several strands of it separated from her skull. Then she turned back and faced Lyra again.

"Come on, Lyra! Let's go!"

Lyra gave one last glance at Darian, then turned to look at Tobias.

"Why did you do that?"

"He attacked me, Lyra," Tobias said gently. "And remember what he said? Remember…this is what he wanted."

Tobias wasn't at all sure he had done the right thing. He easily could've subdued the boy without killing him, just as he had subdued Sabrina and Lucien. But somehow…a quick death seemed to be more in-line with what he wanted. So, Tobias gave it to him. And he wasn't going to make the same mistake and resurrect him again. He was sure of that.

After a few more minutes, the twins stood up and walked away from the scene. Tobias standing over Hunter's sleeping form, a dead, electrocuted teenager, and two unconscious people who seemed to have been blown away from an explosion. Remnants of Darian's car remained scattered throughout the parking lot. The twins broke into a run after leaving the parking lot. Tobias vaguely wondered if they had drivers' licenses or money of any kind, but he realized he had more important matters. That explosion would not go unnoticed for long.

Mages needed to remain in hiding, for their own protection but also for the protection of others. It was too easy for magic to be used and abused in ways that it should not be. War, for example, would be made far deadlier to everyone with magic than without. But even mundane, everyday tasks like public transportation would go away if everyone could teleport. No, the Rebellion was right about one thing: magic was a great power, and great responsibility for the wielder. The Bellwater Mages believed anyone who could use magic should be able to do so, but perhaps that was short-sighted after all. While anyone can use magic, that doesn't mean everyone should use magic. He'd have to have a chat with Aurora about that.

Chapter Sixteen:
...Make a Right?

Tobias tried several times to get Hunter to wake up, to no avail. He had stirred but had instantly fallen back asleep. It seemed Hunter's energy had been waning for a long time. So, Tobias thought it best, for the sake of time, to simply carry him through the air using the wind. The wind carried Hunter, making it look like he was levitating.

The building that stood in front of them looked very familiar to Tobias. It was the same one he and Odion had infiltrated, though it seemed closed. It was the off-season for cruises, Tobias supposed. Though he could hear sirens in the distance; perhaps the Rebellion would be in financial trouble if the government seized their assets here. He didn't think anything of it. Leaving the bodies of Sabrina, Lucien, and Darian behind, he guided Hunter into the building. It was dark, it seemed nobody was working today, yet the door was unlocked. He supposed Sabrina and Lucien must've been in here and had left it unlocked, turning the lights off as they went. With a small snap of his fingers, Tobias locked the door with a small jolt of electricity. This was not to protect him from any Rebellion mages, this was to hopefully slow the police down enough to give him time to search for Aurora and Odion. He was choosing to believe what Lyra had said about the two of them being in here, for he had literally nothing else to go on. If he had to, he thought gruesomely, he could pull an Aurora and take out the entire police force. But he would prefer not to.

The building was dark and difficult to navigate, being largely unfamiliar to Tobias. He remembered that there were several doors down a hallway. He ended up grabbing a flashlight from a nearby security desk and using that to help guide him. He didn't want to turn the big lights on. He was hoping to keep the police out of the building for as long as possible. It would hopefully look like a car explosion had happened in the parking lot, and the police would have little reason to enter the building in the first place. If lights were on inside, that would indicate that there were people inside, and they may be more prone to trying to enter the building to evacuate it.

Tobias had a funny feeling he knew where Aurora and Odion were being kept, and was not disappointed when he found himself at the end of the hall leading down to the locked door where he knew the Rebellion kept its secret files and materials. He turned the door and found it locked but opened it with a small snap of his fingers again. It opened for him with ease.

He guided Hunter down the stairs, taking care to avoid hitting the man's head into the wall or anything. Once at the bottom, he looked around carefully. He could hear, towards the end of the hall, sounds coming that were not present last time. He walked quickly, hoping to preserve his strength as he approached the end of the hall. He held his ear to each door he passed and took a small glance through the window to see if there was anyone inside. It was a windowless door he stopped at, almost at the end of the hall. He tried to open it, but it was locked. When he turned the door handle, he heard a sharp intake of breath from inside, and scrambled as though someone were running away from the door.

Using the same trick he used with the outer door, he unlocked it with a snap of his fingers. His face turned into a face-splitting grin when he saw the occupants of the room: Aurora and Odion.

Aurora was lying on the floor. She seemed unconscious. Rose petals were scattered all around her, and she was covered in cuts, scrapes, and scratches. In the corner, making himself appear as small as possible, was Odion. Tobias' heart sank when he examined him closer; the man appeared to have several burns all over his arms and legs. His usual pristine suit was absent; he wore nothing but underwear and a white undershirt. Even his feet were bare and were covered in blisters. It seemed he had been tortured.

"Odion!"

"To…Tobias?!"

Odion stared at the man in disbelief, then backed away from him.

"Is this another trick?!" he practically screamed.

Tobias blinked. "What? No! It's me, Odion! It's Tobias. We went on an adventure together?"

Odion still seemed skeptical, and outright anxious. Tobias felt sorry for him. He felt like he remembered Aurora saying something to him about Odion struggling with anxiety.

"Come on, we don't have long. Are you…can you walk?"

"Yeah, I suppose."

Odion stood up, his legs shaking. Tobias wasn't sure if they were shaking with fear, excitement, anxiety, or a combination of all three. He frowned at the man.

"Are you okay?"

"Do I look like I'm okay?" he snapped. Tobias was startled at this reaction. Then Odion said, a bit calmer, "No, I'm not okay, Tobias. But you're right. Let's get out of here."

He walked towards Tobias, his pace quickening with every step.

"Hold on," Odion said. "Are we…bringing Aurora?"

"Yes."

Tobias snapped his fingers, and Aurora was scooped up into a small gust of wind, floating alongside Hunter.

"We need to get out of here," Tobias said quickly. "Take a right out the door and go up the stairs. Then I can teleport us to safety."

"Odion?"

This voice was unfamiliar to Tobias. He heard Odion gasp and say, "Marina?!"

A blue-haired, skinny young woman appeared in the doorway. She, too, had several cuts and bruises down her arms and legs.

"What's going on? Where do you think you're going?"

Tobias could tell by Marina's tone that she was not about

to let them just leave. The name sounded familiar to Tobias as well; he felt he remembered Hunter saying something about her at one point but couldn't remember completely.

"We're leaving," Tobias said shortly.

"Who are you?" Marina asked coldly.

"Someone who's going to kill you if you get in our way," Tobias retorted.

"Unfortunately, you're taking my prisoners," Marina responded. "They kept me prisoner, it's only fair I get to keep them prison–"

A small bolt of lightning came down and struck Marina right in the head. She screamed, but it was a short scream until she crumbled to the floor, unconscious.

"Tobias!" Odion gasped. "What'd you do that for?!"

"She was slowing us down?" Tobias snapped as though this were obvious.

"But…"

"Odion, we can talk about this later. Let's go!"

Odion turned and walked away from Marina, towards the door that Tobias had indicated. The two of them walked up the stairs, both Hunter and Aurora ahead of them. Tobias was very interested in hearing what Odion had to say, but they needed to get to safety first. He could already hear movement down the hall from them. Tobias guessed it was the police, though he couldn't be sure. Odion opened the door and stepped outside into the hall. Aurora and Hunter followed him, and Tobias brought up the rear.

Chapter Seventeen: Catching Up is Hard to Do

Tobias, Odion, and the unconscious Aurora and Hunter arrived in a large clearing less than five minutes later. Bellwater Clearing, the exact scene where Tobias and Hunter had fought several months ago. Tobias gasped upon arriving at the clearing and started massaging a stitch in his chest. Odion fared a little bit better, but only just; he had had to support the full weight of Aurora on his shoulders while Tobias helped Hunter to teleport away from the Arcane Rebellion's headquarters. The two men stood, panting for several minutes before the gasps subsided. The two unconscious bodies were laying on the ground, completely still, though both people were obviously breathing.

"So, what happened to you?" Tobias finally asked after both men had caught their breaths.

"You first," Odion snapped. Tobias was startled at this response; Odion seemed upset, almost angry with him. "What the hell happened to you? We thought you had died!"

Taken aback, Tobias explained everything to Odion. He explained how he had gone into this very clearing to think, had been ambushed by Hunter and taken to seclusion, had been held prisoner by Hunter over the last several weeks. He explained how Hunter had allowed everyone to think he was dead for his protection. Conveniently, he left out the part where Hunter was also trying to protect himself from the wrath of Sabrina and

Lucien; he felt Odion didn't need to know that just now. Odion started to interrupt him, but Tobias found it easier to explain once he got going with things, so Tobias simply talked over him until Odion grew quiet again.

He explained how Hunter's cottage had been discovered by Darian, Lyra, and Elena; how the three had managed to overpower Hunter and take them away, back to the Rebellion; and how Sabrina and Lucien discovered Hunter's secret.

"So let me get this straight," Odion almost sighed after Tobias had finally stopped talking, almost half an hour later. "These three teenagers overpowered your 'friend'," he nodded towards Hunter, and Tobias frowned at the emphasis on the word 'friend'. "They took you back to Sabrina and Lucien. They were going to let you go, and you...somehow got your magic back? But I thought your magic had been drained by him?" Once again, he indicated Hunter with pure disgust.

"It had been, Odion," Tobias explained gently. "But remember, acts of love and kindness make the magic come back. I felt...well, Hunter made me feel loved, Odion. That's what prompted my magic to come back."

"How could he make you feel loved?"

"What do you mean?"

"I mean...look, Toby. He kidnapped you. He held you against your will for almost three months, in a cottage. Very little food or water. That's not...normal."

"I know," Tobias said quickly. It was important for Odion to understand that he knew full well what Hunter did wasn't great.

"I am well aware that Hunter acted…well, he made some poor choices–"

"That," Odion interrupted loudly, "Is putting it mildly, Toby. People go to jail for less than what he did to you! Not to mention, he very nearly did kill you, remember?"

Tobias was silent for a moment and turned to face the unconscious man. Of course, Hunter had acted rather rashly. His actions were heinous. Assault, attempted murder, false imprisonment, kidnapping, ongoing mental abuse had all happened to him under the watch of this man. Tobias knew that. And yet…

The thing about Tobias that was both a blessing and a curse was his ability to love. Despite everything that had happened, he still loved Hunter. Not in a romantic sense–he didn't think he could ever love someone like that. No, but he viewed his captor as nearly a brother. Everything the pair of them had been through not only in the last few months, but in the years prior it seemed to flood Tobias' memories, cloud his judgement, and make it impossible to do anything but forgive Hunter. He would not forget everything the man had done to him. But he couldn't pretend he didn't understand it either. "You can have the best intentions in the world, and still do harm" seemed to ring through his mind at the mere sight of Hunter. Hunter had undoubtedly had good intentions and had undoubtedly done harm. And yet, should the harm outweigh the good intentions?

Tobias shook his head. "You don't understand, Odion," he said finally. "Some things…some things you just need to forgive people for."

"Help me to understand then, Tobias," Odion responded

coldly, and Tobias registered the lack of 'Toby' that was coming out of Odion's mouth. "Help me to understand how you can forgive this monster for everything he did to you?!" Tobias thought for a split second Odion was going to kick Hunter's unconscious body, but this was proven false; Odion seemed to think twice about doing so, possibly because he felt Tobias might attack him if he hurt his precious Hunter. Tobias sighed.

"It's not that I completely and irrevocably forgive him, Odion," Tobias explained gently. "But sometimes…sometimes holding a grudge is worse than just moving on from it. Hunter did terrible things, there is no denying it. Our friendship will absolutely suffer for a while, possibly forever, because of the things he did to me. He did them because he thought he was saving me from…" he turned his attention, for the first time in a while, to the woman lying feet from him: Aurora. Odion followed Tobias' eyes and narrowed his own at the sight.

"I told you there was something up with her, Tobias. Remember? When she strangled that girl with a flower? And you should've seen the things she did to Marina."

"Who's Marina?"

"That girl you electrocuted back there," Odion snapped. "Why'd you have to do that, by the way?"

A thought seemed to click in Tobias's mind. "What did she do to you, Odion?"

"What do you mean?"

"What did Marina do to you and Aurora?"

157

Odion was speechless for a bit, then he said sheepishly, "We deserved it, Tobias."

"Deserved what?"

"She did to us what we did to her. We—Aurora and I—had captured her and tried to get her to give us information on you. But Sabrina and Lucien turned the tables on us. They found and captured us, saved Marina, and then held us hostage."

"You seem pretty upset that I saved you from her."

"She didn't deserve it!" Odion snapped. "She didn't do anything wrong! We were the ones in the wrong! That's the difference here, Toby. You didn't do anything to Hunter. We did bad things to Marina. Aurora tortured her with vines and thorns trying to get her to tell us where you were, but like you said, Hunter—" he scoffed again at the mere mention of the man's name, "--you did nothing to him, and yet he got you shot, then he attacked you and held you prisoner!"

Tobias was startled to see tears in Odion's eyes.

"You...you're really upset about this, Odion."

Odion nodded. "We spent...weeks...looking for you, bro. And having to deal with her—" he indicated this time towards Aurora, "--it wasn't easy."

"Did you just bro me?"

Odion chuckled. "I suppose I did. Been hanging around Foxton too much, I suppose. He's living with me now."

"That's a dangerous game, Odion."

"Yeah, well, never mind that. Aurora is...well, she's another one that I'm not sure what you're doing with her, Toby."

"She saved my life."

"Yes, but all the same. She's chaotic, and sadistic. Not someone you should trust, Toby."

Tobias didn't say anything. He turned to face the two people he valued more than anything else in the world. The truth was, Odion had very valid points. Hunter had committed serious crimes in his quest to protect Tobias. Noble or not, that's not something he could just ignore. And Aurora, from the sounds of it, wasn't much better; she had also done some shady stuff in her quest to find Tobias. He sighed at the irony of the situation. Hunter and Aurora, who couldn't stand one another, had the same end goal all this time: protecting him. He thought maybe he should tell them about this observation when they woke up.

It seemed he wouldn't have long to wait until they awakened; both Hunter and Aurora were stirring. Tobias wasn't sure what he would end up doing; he hadn't anticipated the two of them waking up at the same time. He also wasn't sure what would happen when they woke up and saw the other. He hoped a fight wasn't about to break out between them; he wasn't sure he or Odion had it in them to break up a fight between two powerful mages.

Hunter sat up first and looked around wildly.

"What happened?" were the first words out of his mouth. It seemed he was on edge. Tobias stared down at him, but Odion spoke first.

"Tobias saved you, you dolt."

Hunter glared around and saw Odion. "What do you–" his sentence cut off as he saw Tobias.

"What...what happened, Toby? I remember those kids fighting us–"

He turned as Aurora started making more noise. He snarled in her direction, evidently not pleased to see her.

"What is she doing here?"

"I could ask the same to you," Aurora snapped back, rubbing her back; it seemed she was in quite a bit of pain. "Why am I on the ground? Where–Toby?!"

She jumped up in surprise and winced as she felt the pain in her back again. Tobias walked over to her and wrapped her up in a hug.

"Thank you," he said softly. "For trying to find me."

The two of them held each other for a few minutes until they broke apart. This seemed to stabilize Aurora a bit; she could now stand on her own without falling over, at least.

"What happened to you?" she asked in barely more than a whisper. He ignored her. Instead, he went to Hunter. He held out a hand and helped Hunter to his feet. Then, he wrapped his best friend in a hug that, like it did for Aurora, seemed to give him some stability on his feet. Odion glared at Hunter the whole time this happened, and Aurora too narrowed her eyes at the sight of this, but neither of them said anything. The two men broke apart after a few minutes.

"Thanks, Toby."

Tobias nodded, then turned to face the group. "I am going to explain what happened to me. Then we are going to all go back to the way things were before Hunter left. There will be no grudges held, there will be no more fighting. We are all on the same team. Some mistakes were made, we will all get over it from this point forward."

Hunter, Aurora and Odion all looked outraged and appalled at Tobias' words. But Tobias held up a warning finger.

"We will move past this," he said firmly. "I insist."

Recognizing defeat, the three adults grew silent as they watched Tobias. The man began pacing as he explained, once again and in great detail, everything that had happened to him between Hunter nearly killing him and he himself saving the quartet.

The three adults listened intently, but as Tobias got to the end, Aurora laughed.

"Hunter nearly killed you again, then kidnapped and falsely imprisoned you? Shall I do the honors, Toby?"

A flower shot itself out of a nearby flower bush and wrapped itself tightly around Hunter's neck. Hunter snapped his fingers, and the flower burned away effortlessly.

"I'm not some teenage girl you can threaten with tricks like that, you stupid old hag."

It looked like Aurora was not done, however. On the contrary, now the ground itself seemed to be attacking Hunter. The ground shook underneath the four of them, threatening to swallow them into a large crevice that seemed to be appearing right underneath Hunter's feet.

But it was Tobias who stepped in and snapped his fingers this time. Not only did Hunter zoom up into the air, away from harm, Aurora was struck by a small bolt of lightning squarely between her eyeballs at the same time. She screamed in pain, the ground stopped trembling, and she turned towards Tobias, seething.

"Let's talk about what you did, Aurora."

"Excuse me?"

"You are not innocent here either, Aurora. Attacking students, police, and Odion tells me you also held someone hostage in hopes of getting information from them."

Aurora turned pale and shook her head wildly.

"Toby...I can't believe we are discussing this. Don't you know what he did to you?"

She sounded so much like Odion, it was almost funny, Tobias thought.

"You're just as bad as he is. Worse, in some ways, Aurora. You're not willing to admit you're in the wrong here."

"Because I'm not."

Tobias and Aurora, who had always gotten along so well with each other, stood facing each other, glaring. Hunter looked as though Christmas had come early. Odion stood in the shadows, looking from one to the next, his expression neutral.

"Aurora," Tobias started, with the air of someone explaining that two plus two did indeed equal four. "I appreciate everything you've done for me. More than you will ever know. But you went well over the line in your efforts to save me. Surely you can agree with that?"

"Absolutely not, Tobias." Aurora was now shaking with rage. "I did everything I was supposed to do, Tobias. All in the name of protecting you. He–" she pointed at Hunter, "--decided he was going to kill you, failed, and it seems as though you've forgiven him! Oh, but I'm not surprised in the slightest, Tobias! You're a fool, you always have been. You love too easily, you forgive too quickly, and you will always be a doormat for anyone to walk all over and take advantage of whenever they need something! You may be great at magic, but that's meaningless when prior actions have no consequences whatsoever to you!"

"Except they do," Tobias interrupted. "Your prior actions have consequences, Aurora."

"And what of Hunter's prior actions?"

"We are talking about you right now–"

"Oh, don't you dare try that trick on me, Tobias Thornfield!" Aurora was practically shrieking now. "I taught you everything there is to know about being a teacher, and you will not pull that card on me when I'm the one who taught it to you! 'We are talking about you right now' is for students who don't do their homework for the umpteenth time and then try to make it seem like you're picking favorites. That's not going to work on me! Not in this case. You are choosing to forgive his gross misdeeds and to condemn me for mine. No, I will not stand for this, Tobias!" She stomped her foot in anger, and the ground shook once again underneath all three men this time. Tobias stood his ground, Hunter watched in amazement, and Odion sunk deeper into the shadows.

"I will not forgive you unless you admit that you were in the wrong, Aurora." Tobias spoke firmly.

Three huge thorns appeared out of the ground at these words, and slammed down on Tobias, Hunter, and Odion simultaneously. Hunter alone expected it, put a shield of fire up around himself, and his thorn evaporated at once. Tobias was thrown backwards and slammed into a tree. Odion slammed into the ground hard and immediately began bleeding profusely. In a moment of clarity, Hunter made the split-second decision that he needed to help Tobias and Odion instead of stopping Aurora. Out of the corner of his eye, he saw her teleport away. He ran to Odion first, who was closer and seemed more gravely injured. Hunter snapped his fingers, and the thorn suffocating Odion burned away just like the flower had burned around Hunter. Odion started coughing, hard. Hunter picked him up and gave him a quick bear hug, then carried him as he ran over to Tobias. Tobias seemed more shaken than anything; it appeared he had put up a small shield around himself not a moment too soon that had deflected most of the attack. The thorn had launched itself at Tobias for a second time, but Tobias struck it down with a powerful bolt of lightning and it disintegrated just as Hunter's had.

"Toby!" Hunter cried. Odion was holding on to him, slowing him down, but Tobias ran to meet them halfway. The two men put the youngest man between them and hugged it out. Within seconds, Odion was fully recovered. Then they broke apart.

"What made you see reason, Toby?" asked Hunter, smiling widely.

Tobias raised his eyebrows. "Don't think you're out of the woods, Hunter. You're no angel."

Hunter punched him on the arm, then repeated his question. "You finally saw her for who she is, Toby. Why?"

Tobias turned away. Then he said quietly, "I really thought she'd admit she did wrong."

Chapter Eighteen: The Search Begins

Tobias, Hunter, and Odion returned to Odion's apartment where they were greeted by Foxton and Finnian. The looks of shock on their faces when they saw their old teacher–and the man who had supposedly killed him–did not surprise or disappoint Tobias. Odion called a special meeting of the Bellwater Mages–a teacher's union meeting–and Matilda Carrington, Agatha O'Connor, Foxton, and Finnian heard the story that Tobias had told Aurora, Hunter, and Odion.

"So, Sabrina and Lucien were the moles, and Aurora ended up going crazy." Agatha summarized at the end of his story.

"I guess that's one way to put it," Tobias shrugged.

"But what happens now?" Matilda asked the group at large. "Aurora was Principal of Bellwater Academy, Sabrina and Lucien were both teachers. This will not go unnoticed. Parents will hear all about it."

"Undoubtedly," Tobias agreed. "We also need to figure out what we're going to do about our group of magic users. Someone will need to take the reins from Sabrina and Lucien–"

"You."

It was Hunter who spoke. And no one objected.

"Me?" asked Tobias, startled.

"You're the only option, really," Odion agreed, startling Tobias even more.

"It's an easy pick," concurred Matilda.

"You're the best man for the job," Agatha concluded.

"No, surely Agatha—"

"I'm an old lady, Tobias. What do you expect me to do, break my other hip trying to keep us together?"

"Honestly, I'm glad that Miss Wildwood is gone," Foxton chimed in. "She was kind of…crazy."

Tobias sighed. "Okay. Fine. Temporarily, I will take over the Bellwater Mages. But what about the school? Percival fired me and reported me to the state licensing board. I can't just go back to teaching there."

"Actually, Aurora told me he never actually reported you to the state," Odion corrected him. "Besides, I don't think parents will think anything of it. They'll be much more concerned about the fact that we are on our second principal and have lost several teachers all in the course of one semester. Not even a full school year!"

There were several murmurs of agreement around the room. Tobias sighed again.

"Okay. I will go back to Bellwater then. Hunter," he turned to face the man, who had been standing in the shadows behind

167

him. Everyone around the room tensed. Tobias noticed this, and rather than finishing his thought, asked Hunter, "Please explain what's going to happen to you now."

Hunter rose himself up to his full height, then said quickly, "I'm recommitting myself to the Bellwater Mages. I'm so sorry for all the trouble I caused. I hope you can find it in your hearts to forgive me, and to give me another chance."

There were looks of outrage and doubt around the room at this. Tobias chimed in.

"Forgiveness and trust are earned, Hunter. Prove to us that you deserve our forgiveness."

"How will I go about doing that?"

"Simple," Tobias retorted. "You will find Aurora, bring her back here–alive–and help her see that what she did was wrong. Do this, and we'll know we can trust you. Oh, and you're bringing Odion."

"What?" Odion sounded outraged.

"You're going with Hunter," Tobias repeated firmly. "You need to learn more about magic, don't you? And I need someone I can trust to keep an eye on Hunter. Plus, you know more about Aurora at this point than Hunter does. He needs you, Odion."

"Sound logic," Agatha said, sounding impressed.

Tobias turned to face Hunter, and said very slowly and deliberately, "Odion is in charge of this mission, Hunter. Do you understand me?"

Hunter looked slightly disappointed but also like he had been expecting it. "Yes, sir. I do."

"In your own words, tell me what I just told you to do."

"We are to go find Aurora and bring her back here alive. Odion is to accompany me, and he is in charge because he knows Aurora better than I do."

"And because I'm not a psychopath," Odion offered.

"Give it time," Hunter snapped back. Tobias held back a laugh, there were a few other chuckles around the room.

"What are we going to do about Sabrina and Lucien?" Matilda asked Tobias. "They've been arrested, as well as a blue-haired girl." This caught Odion's attention. "We can't just let the police keep them locked up, nor can we let them break out of prison on their own. What's your plan, Tobias?"

Tobias nodded, then said, "I am going to deal with them personally. And," he turned to face Foxton. "If you're willing, I'd like you to accompany me."

Foxton looked surprised. "Me? Why me?"

"You're a senior, aren't you? You're almost done with your senior year. We can arrange for you to graduate early and begin your study of magic. With me."

"Do you think having him hunt down Sabrina and Lucien by himself is the wisest move, Tobias?" Matilda asked, sounding doubtful.

"He will not be by himself, Matilda," Tobias replied calmly. He turned to face the group. "He'll be with me."

Connect with Denis James

Denis James has a true passion for all things mental health related. A (recovering) chronic depression and severe anxiety patient, Denis James writes with the intention of helping others who may be where he once was. When not writing, Denis can be seen teaching in his community (he currently teaches computer technology skills), nerding out (his favorite fandoms include Pokémon, Harry Potter, Yu-Gi-Oh, and Kingdom Hearts), planning travel, or being home with his family.

Connect with Denis James:

Facebook: Denis James – Writer
Instagram: denisjameswriter
Patreon: Denis James – Writer

Made in the USA
Monee, IL
20 July 2025

21161711R00104